Murder at Merisham Lodge

MISS HART AND MISS HUNTER INVESTIGATE

Celina Grace

This book is for Katie D'Arcy, with love.

Chapter One

I'M NOT ASHAMED TO SAY that I screamed when the body fell at my feet. In fact, it almost fell *on* my feet, but I managed to stagger backwards. Instead of receiving the full force of impact, my one pair of decent shoes received a stippling of blood across the toes, spattering the leather in a string of glossy red beads.

There was an exclamation and I looked up, furious.

"Sorry! Sorry, miss." One of the men I'd seen working on the estate hurried towards me, his shotgun hanging loosely from his hand. "I didn't see you there."

By now he had reached me and we both looked down at the body of the magpie, its black and white wings a monochrome splash against the dusty grass.

By now, I hoped I'd recovered a little poise. "You startled me," I said inadequately, trying to stop my voice from shaking. The man hung his head a little. He was younger than I'd first thought, about thirty-five, his skin tanned and weathered from all the work he did outdoors. "What on Earth are you doing, shooting magpies, anyway?" I added in a more normal tone.

"Ah, they'll take the young chicks if they find them, miss," he said. He stooped and picked up the body of the bird. "Not as bad as the kestrels, though, but we've still got orders to shoot them if we see them around the breeding grounds."

"I see," I said. I looked at my shoes again and tutted.

The man almost blushed. "Let me help you there, miss," he mumbled and bent and tore up a handful of grass. Before I could stop him, he had wiped the blood from the toes of my shoes.

"Thank you," I said, my own cheeks now scarlet. I was half thinking that he'd done that just to get a good look at my legs. He clambered back onto his feet and stood back a little, to let me pass by.

"You work up at the kitchens, don't you?" he said, just as I was walking away.

"Yes, I'm the undercook," I said with dignity and perhaps just a touch of 'so I'm higher in the servants' hierarchy than *you*' in my voice.

I'm not sure he got the message. He grinned and said, "Well, I'll have some lovely birds for you to cook up soon, miss."

I said nothing but gave him a cool nod and went on my way.

It was summer's last gasp, September 1930; the very tail end of the good weather. It was a good season in Derbyshire when it was still warm, with the chill of autumn just around the corner but not yet felt. The leaves on the trees were just beginning to be touched with colour, turning yellow here and there within the mass of green. The sun still had some real warmth behind it. Though I was supposed to be hurrying back – my afternoon off ended abruptly at four o'clock – somehow I just couldn't seem to make my feet move faster than a dawdle. I followed the footpath that skirted the edge of the Merisham estate, winding through the oak and beech trees. Halfway along the path, I had to clamber over a stile, a little awkwardly in my long skirt, before the path led me across a field, past the chattering little brook that crossed the corner, over another stile and finally onto the road that eventually led to the back gate of the lodge.

Merisham Lodge had been in Lord Cartwright's family for over a hundred years. My friend, Verity, had told me so when she persuaded me to apply for a position here.

"It's a big old place," she told me and then added hastily after seeing me flinch, "but not *that* old – not as old as Asharton Manor. The family keeps it for shooting parties and for their summer residence, normally. They're going up a little early, this year, and so they'll need a full set of staff..."

"I don't know, V," I said. "Is it very isolated? I don't think I could stand that again."

Verity hastened to reassure me. "It's only a mile from the village, and you're less than five miles from Buxton. It's nothing like Asharton Manor, believe me, Joan."

"Hmmm," I said, not entirely convinced, but then I trusted Verity. After all, what other choice did I have? It wasn't as if there were hundreds of jobs out there for a partly-trained kitchen maid, or at least not so many in places that I would actually want to work. If I took a position at Merisham Lodge, I'd be working in the same house as Verity. We might even get to share a room. It wasn't as if I particularly liked the place where I was working at that time; it was a doctor's house in Kilburn. It had been one of the places I'd applied for in a panic after I left Asharton Manor.

"The food's good, and you get a decent amount of time off," Verity said encouragingly.

"What about *them*?" I didn't have to elaborate any further. Verity knew whom I meant.

"Oh, he's a bugger," she said cheerfully. "And Madam's just as bad. But believe me, Joan, you won't come into contact with them very often, so you don't have to worry."

"Hmmm," I said once more, but that was just for show. By that time, I'd already made up my mind.

My first sight of the lodge hadn't exactly been

encouraging. I'd met the housekeeper, Mrs Anstells, in London to be interviewed. I had actually met her before, as Verity had worked for the family for years. Of course, Verity had also put a good word in for me, and I had a good reference from my last position at Asharton Manor (probably the only positive thing to come out of the whole ghastly experience). I was pleased but not greatly surprised when I was offered the position. I'd taken the train up the following week and prepared to walk the couple of miles from Merisham Station to the lodge. My trunk hadn't been that big but it seemed to get heavier and heavier, the further I plodded. Of course it *would* start raining before I got more than fifty yards. I trudged on through the downpour, thinking what a fine sight I'd look when I actually got to the lodge; more like a drowned rat than a professional servant.

As I walked, I remembered the first sight I'd had of Asharton Manor and what a shock it had been. It had seemed like a palace to me, newly arrived from grey old London. What a fine sight it had been – and how deceptive the appearance was. It wasn't particularly cold, despite the rain, but I still shivered at the memories.

By then I had become more accustomed fine houses and the lodge didn't look all that awe-inspiring, especially as I could only glimpse it through a curtain of falling rain. It looked handsome enough, I suppose; solid, well-built, and surrounded by some fine lawns and well-tended gardens. I had walked on round the back, of course, and rang the rather rusty bell affixed to the wall by the back door, wondering what my fellow servants would be like.

Today, the house looked very different in the spring sunshine. In high spirits, after my walk and the few hours I'd had to please myself, I wiped my feet on the boot-scraper by the back door and went on into the kitchen.

"Oh, Joan, you're back. Good." The cook, Mrs Watling, darted back and forth between stoves, as was her wont. I'd never met someone quite so blessed with energy – she made me, some twenty years her junior, feel quite tired. "Had a nice afternoon?"

"Lovely, thank you," I said with feeling. I liked my job well enough, and Mrs Watling was a good and patient person to work for, but all the same, a job is a job and after a few hours of freedom, it was always rather melancholy to come back to reality with a bump. I tried to shake off the feeling. It helped that the kitchen windows were flung wide and the sunshine and fresh spring air flooded through into the kitchen.

As kitchens go, it was actually quite a pleasant place to work. The whole room had been modernised some years before and we had, wonder of wonders, a gas stove as well as the range. The 'pop' of the gas as it lit had scared me stiff at first – I was sure we'd all be blown to kingdom come – but as was usual, it was amazing how quickly I got used to it and soon became rather blasé about striking a match and lighting it. The floor was tiled with smooth red ceramic tiles, such a pleasant change from the usual pitted and marked flagstones that needed a hearty scrubbing every day before they looked clean.

"Joan, go and change, there's a good girl. They'll be wanting tea at half four, and I'll need you to cut sandwiches." Mrs Watling scraped a load of carrot peelings into the stock pot with a flourish. "There's the ginger cake that needs eating as well. That and scones should be enough, I would have thought."

I nodded obediently and made for the servants' stairs. Those stairs irritated me, as they had done in every house I'd been in that had them. It wasn't enough that we had to run around after these people, catering to their every whim and often receiving nothing but scorn in return, but that we had to do all that whilst remaining as invisible as we possibly could. I mean, God forbid that we were able to use the hallowed steps of the main staircase. I stomped on upwards, my good mood of the morning dimming more the further up the stairs I went.

One of the good things about working at Merisham Lodge was that I had indeed been able to share a room with Verity. It wasn't the way things were normally done, the undercook and a lady's maid sharing a room, but, in her usual way, Verity had charmed Mrs Anstells around into thinking that it was a good idea. I wondered whether Verity would be there now, but it didn't seem likely. Verity was lady's maid to the daughter of the house, Dorothy, and would very likely now be cleaning her jewellery or mending her underwear, or making up a beauty potion for her mistress to use later. I knocked on the door of our room, just in case, but only silence met me. Never mind. I'd see Verity at dinner time, and we'd be able to have a good old chinwag then.

I hung up my skirt and blouse and pulled on my uniform. Standing in front of the little mirror, which hung on the far wall above the narrow table we used as a dressing table, I peered at my dim reflection. I tried to scrape back my hair until it was entirely hidden under my cap. It was difficult, as I had to virtually festoon my very thick, long hair with hairpins before it consented to do what it was told. As always, I wondered whether I would ever be bold enough to have it cut short, like Dorothy Drew wore hers, in a daring flapper bob. But then, when you're rich and young and beautiful, you can carry off a style like that. "Dorothy would look good in an old sack," I remember Verity saying once, and I had to agree. Fleetingly, I wondered whether Dorothy would be considered *quite* so beautiful if she hadn't been *quite* so rich.

My hair safely stowed away under my cap, I picked up a clean apron and a clean pair of cuffs and made my way back downstairs, hurrying as I caught

sight of the clock. I hastened into the kitchen, washed my hands, and began sawing at a loaf of bread. Cucumber sandwiches and meat paste, perhaps... Mrs Watling backed out of the larder, her hands full of eggs, and gave me an approving nod.

"Don't forget the ginger cake," was all she said before she sped off in the direction of the wine cellar.

The sandwiches cut, the ginger cake placed on a cake tray, and the jam and butter carefully decanted into separate pots, I hastily arranged the scones on a plate and added the linen napkins. I could hear the drawing room bell jangling away out in the passage but nobody appeared. Cursing under my breath, I went out in the corridor, wondering if I should shout. Where was everybody? I knew Nora, one of the two parlourmaids of the house, was out on her afternoon off – I'd even seen her in the village and we'd exchanged smiles from across the street – but Nancy should have been here. It was almost quarter to five and the bell for the drawing room was even now bouncing up and down on its hook. I cursed a little louder, whipped off my dirty apron, and picked up the tray.

I pounded up the back stairs to the ground floor, manoeuvred my way through the door to the hallway, and then hurried along towards the drawing room, tray chinking and clinking in my hands. I caught sight of myself in the enormous gilt-framed mirror that hung on one side of the hallway and groaned inwardly. I was scarlet in the face, tiny beads of sweat garlanding my nose. While the apron I'd discarded in the kitchen had kept the worst of the muck off my dress, there were still enough spots and splashes and stains all over me to make me look like something that could have been dragged up from the cellar.

Nobody will even notice you, I told myself reassuringly, and sure enough, once I'd knocked and was bid to enter, I might as well have been invisible. I set the tea tray on the round table by the window, just as it was always placed for this daily ritual.

The whole family was gathered in the drawing room: Lord and Lady Cartwright, Lord Cartwright's son, Duncan, and Lady Cartwright's daughter, Dorothy. Lord Cartwright's social secretary, Rosalind Makepeace, was also there, sitting quietly by herself over to one side of the room. I looked at her quickly before looking just as quickly away. She intrigued me: she was good looking, in a way that was the antithesis of Dorothy Drew's showy beauty. Rosalind's face had something more subtle. *Still waters run deep* was the phrase that occurred to me then. I thought she had a kind of foreign look to her, without being able to say exactly what I meant by that. Perhaps it was her black hair, glossy and smooth as jet, or the sharpness of her cheekbones. Duncan Cartwright was seated next to Rosalind, but he was turned quite sharply away from her, leaning towards Dorothy. As usual, they were laughing and joking together, the cigarettes in their hands sending up twining blue tendrils of smoke that partly veiled their faces. He *was* good-looking, I thought, that was undeniable, but all the same, I didn't much like his face. There was something a little cruel around his mouth, and while he seemed to be always smiling, it never seemed to reach his eyes.

Lady Cartwright approached the tea table. She was a tall woman, with a figure that could have, from the back, been taken as that of a girl thirty years younger. From the front, the illusion fell away. She was hard-faced, with a manner that was superficially charming but – as all we maids had experienced – a temper beneath it that could be quite frightening.

I braced myself to speak to her. "Will that be all, my lady?" I murmured in what I hoped was the right respectful kind of voice.

"Yes, yes," she said impatiently, dismissing me. As I left the room, Albert, one of the footmen, hurried past me into the drawing room. Good, he could serve them, because I certainly wasn't going to. Thankfully, I pulled the door shut behind me and hurried back downstairs to the kitchen. At least there I didn't have to face any of *them*.

There were only three of them to dinner that

11

night, Lord and Lady Cartwright and Duncan, so that made for a relatively peaceful afternoon's work for me and Mrs Watling. I had been hoping to be able to have a chat with Verity at the servants' evening meal, but she'd virtually bolted her food and rushed back upstairs, signalling over the table to me with her eyebrows as she left the room. Long practice had made me adept at reading Verity's mobile face. Those eyebrow movements meant that she had a long night's work ahead of her – *damn it to hell*, I heard her voice say inside my head, and grinned – probably because Dorothy was dining out, and Verity would have to wait up for her.

Normally, it was me who got to bed late, unless Verity had to do what she was doing this evening. It was quite a novelty for me to be sitting up in bed, reading my book, with Verity's bed on the other side of the room empty. I'd turned it down for her and slipped one of the stone hot water bottles between the sheets. That was the first thing she remarked on when she finally came into the room at past midnight, when I was virtually nodding off over my book.

"Oh, bless you, Joanie, that's so kind of you." Verity sat, or rather collapsed, onto the edge of her bed. Her face was pale with fatigue, the normal vivid colour of her hair somehow dimmed. She rubbed her face. "God, I'm all of a heap."

"It's so late," I said, yawning. "It's too bad of Dorothy to make you wait up so late."

"Oh, I'm used to it by now," Verity said, beginning to strip off her clothes. "I'm not going to wash, I'm too bloody tired."

"Where had she been tonight?"

"A party somewhere." Verity pulled her nightdress on over her head and sat down again to roll her stockings off. She gave a tired giggle. "She rolled in just as drunk as a lord. She'll have such a head in the morning."

"Humph." I waited until Verity had got into bed and then turned down the oil lamp. "It's all right for some, isn't it?"

I could hear the bedsprings of Verity's mattress clink and chime as she got comfortable. "Well, who's to say we can't do the same? When's your next day off? If it coincides with mine, we could go into town. Have cocktails."

I laughed. "Don't be ridiculous, V."

I could hear her giggle again faintly and then give a much bigger yawn. "Yes, I know. Lord, I'm tired. I must sleep. Night, Joanie."

"Good night." I lay there for a moment, staring into the blackness. I always tried to stay awake a little longer if I could – it was the only time I ever had peace and quiet and time to try and organise my thoughts – but, as usual, it was a hopeless task. The last thing I remembered was the peaceful sound of Verity's breathing before sleep claimed me.

Chapter Two

IT WAS ELEVEN O'CLOCK BY the time I got to finally sit down the next morning. I'd cleared away the last of the breakfast things and seated myself at the table with a pile of potatoes and a vegetable peeler. I didn't mind peeling things – it was monotonous enough work but you could think about other things at the same time. I was pleased when Verity appeared in the kitchen doorway with a pile of clothing in her hands.

"Sewing?" I asked.

Verity nodded. "I've been putting it off, but now we can sit and chat, it won't seem so bad."

"I'll make us some tea," I said, putting aside a half peeled potato and getting up.

Just as I was filling the kettle, there was a knock at the kitchen door. Wiping my hands on my apron, I went to open it.

There was a man outside, a stranger. He was rather smartly dressed for a tradesman and carried his hat in his hand. He was young, probably not more than twenty-five or so, and rather brown.

I raised my eyebrow interrogatively. "May I help you?"

The man shifted from foot to foot. By this time, Verity had looked up from her mending and when she saw who it was, she jumped up with an exclamation.

"Good morning, sir," she said, rushing up to stand beside me at the door. "How may we help?"

So, he merited a 'sir', did he? I let Verity push forward a little.

"Hello, Verity," said the man. "I'm just here to see the mater. She's not expecting me." For a moment, he looked almost shifty. "You couldn't show me up to my room and let the old girl know I've arrived, could you?"

Verity bobbed a curtsey. "Of course, sir. Do come with me."

I watched her whisk the man through the kitchen and out to the passageway beyond. After a moment, I heard what was probably their feet walking overhead as they made for the main staircase.

I sat back down at the table again, frowning. Who on Earth had that been? Clearly he was some part of the gentry – perhaps even part of the family. So why in the world had he come to the servants' entrance and not rung the doorbell of the main house, as anyone else of that status would? It was a puzzle that I turned over in my head as I picked up my peeler and slowly began to divest the potatoes of their jackets.

I'd almost finished by the time Verity came back again.

"Who was that?" I asked as soon as she'd sat back down.

She rolled her eyes. "That was Lady Eveline's son, Peter Drew. He's the son of her first husband. Dorothy's brother."

"I haven't seen him before," I commented, beginning to slice the peeled potatoes.

"No, well, he's not often here. He and his mum don't get along brilliantly. She thinks he's a – well, a wastrel. He only turns up here when he needs some money."

"And Lady Eveline gives it to him?"

Verity smiled cynically. "Not without a screaming row, normally."

I raised my eyebrows. "Is he married?"

"No. Bit of a scoundrel, I think, judging from some of Dorothy's remarks." Verity bit off the thread she was holding. "Sounds like he takes after his father."

"In what way?"

"Well, *he* was a bit of a rogue, by all accounts. Dalliances with actresses and so forth." I raised my eyebrows again and Verity grinned. Her family was connected with the theatre and she knew quite well what some people thought of those in the acting profession. "As it was," she went on, "He got drunk and fell in front of an omnibus one night and that was that. Of course, it was sad for Dorothy and Peter. I mean, he *was* their father."

I tipped the sliced potatoes in a bowl of cold water and shook the salt cellar over it. "So Duncan Cartwright isn't Lady Eveline's son?"

Verity rolled her eyes. "No, Joanie, you *know* that. Remember? Lord Cartwright was married before and his wife died, about a year before he married Lady E."

It was true Verity probably had told me that before but, to be honest, I had little time to worry about remembering the ins and outs of the family. It wasn't as if I came into contact with them much (thankfully), unlike Verity. I suppose she had to know who was who and what was what.

Verity began neatly folding the mended clothing. She had a very steady hand and could make tiny, neat stitches, something I'd never managed to master. She'd trained herself in mending lace, a useful skill for a lady's maid to have, but then Verity was a fiend for self-improvement. "I'm a lifelong student," she told me once, when I caught her poring over an encyclopaedia in the library at Asharton Manor.

Asharton Manor. I caught myself in an involuntary shudder, something that often happened when I remembered the accursed place. It had been

17

cursed, I was sure of it. I wasn't just being fanciful. I remembered the clearing in the forest and the haunted feel of the woods surrounding the house. I remembered, too, the pale shape of the body in the bed, the greyish tinge to her skin, as if she'd walked through a room full of cobwebs.

Verity looked up sharply. "Joan? Are you all right?"

I shook myself back to reality. "Fine. I'm fine." It wasn't like me to brood, but sometimes the memories caught me unawares. Now, how about that cup of tea?"

"Ooh, yes. That would be lovely."

I put the kettle on the hob and lit the gas. "How was Dorothy's head this morning?"

Verity chuckled. She had a lovely, gurgling laugh that always made you want to join in. "Sore! I had to fetch her aspirin by the pound." She finished folding the clothes and began to stack them in a pile. "I think she's got a new beau. She had a card from a Simon Snailer in her handbag and she *never* keeps cards, normally."

"'Simon Snailer!'" I poured out the tea for us both. "She won't want to marry *him*. Imagine being Mrs Dorothy Snailer."

We both laughed at that. "What's he like?" I asked, curious despite myself.

"No idea. I haven't accompanied her out for a bit, I don't know who she's been seeing lately." She picked up the stack of clothing. "Anyway, I'd better get these back upstairs and put away."

"Have your tea first."

"Of course. You do look after me well, Joanie."

"Someone's got to." We smiled at each other. Verity and I had met when we were both small girls, in the orphanage where we both grew up. She was from a high-born family fallen on hard times; I most definitely was not. We had liked each other from the start and now she was my oldest and dearest friend.

I drained my cup and washed it up. Verity said goodbye and went out with the pile of clothing. I began to prepare the soup for the evening meal, quite a complicated one with white fish and various vegetables and herbs. I think I was quite content then, thinking about nothing more than the work I had to do but knowing that it was all under control so far. It was a sunny day and beams of light poured through the large windows, such a pleasant change to some of the kitchens I'd worked in. Mrs Watling came in from her trip to the village and nodded approval at seeing me well employed.

Once the soup was well underway, I stood back and stretched a little, easing my aching back. It was then I noticed a white object over on the floor by the door. Verity had dropped one of Dorothy's chemises as she left the room.

"I'm just going to take this up to Verity," I told Mrs Watling, who nodded again.

"You'll need to make the stuffing for the duck, but that can wait until you get back," she said, whisking in and out of the pantry with her hands full of tins and jars.

I took the servants' stairs, of course. Dorothy's room was on the second floor, so at least it wasn't too much of a climb, unlike at the end of the day when I had to trudge up to the attic floor on tired legs. The servants' door to the second floor was one of those concealed ones, right at the end of the corridor. I closed it behind me quietly and made my way down the hallway.

Raised voices behind one of the doors made me pause. I realised they were coming from Lady Eveline's room – it was her talking, loud and hard, and a man's voice too. I didn't recognise it for a moment and then I realised it was her son, the one who'd arrived this morning, Peter Drew.

"You're just like your father," Lady Eveline said. There was a sneer in her voice, apparent even to me on the other side of the door. "Lazy, useless, and grasping. If you think I'm going to bail you out yet again, you've got another think coming."

Peter spoke then. "I know you've never had much opinion of me, Mother. Not that I can't say the feeling's mutual—"

"How dare you speak to me like that?"

"How dare I? Oh, I dare, all right, mother. And if you're not going to help me, I can think of a few people who might be very interested to hear one or two things about you—"

I was holding my breath and the blood thumped in my ears. I was dying to hear what Peter would say next but I never got the chance. I heard a door opening down the corridor and nearly jumped out of my skin. Hurrying past the door, I swerved into the next room, which was Dorothy's.

Verity was there, folding clothes into the chest of drawers by the adjoining wall. She gave me a wry glance as I panted into the room.

"Going at it hammer and tongs, aren't they?" She inclined her head towards the wall, where the hard angry voices of Lady Cartwright and Peter were still audible. "Told you it always happens when he turns up."

I held out the chemise. "I brought this up for you, you dropped it in the kitchen."

"Oh, thank you, Joanie. I mustn't lose that one, it's French silk." She took it from me and placed it neatly in the top drawer. I sat down on Dorothy's bed. Her room was so lovely: white and feminine and stuffed full of beautiful furniture and paintings and clothes. I got up and went to the wardrobe to gaze hungrily at her lovely dresses.

There was the emphatic slam of the bedroom door in the room next to us and then the sound of footsteps stamping away. Verity and I looked at one another and I bit down on the smile that wanted to show.

Dorothy's own door opened and I leapt away from the wardrobe, expecting it to be Lady Cartwright. But it was Dorothy herself, wrapped in a white satin dressing gown with large embroidered poppies on the lapels.

"Oh, hullo, Joan," she said amiably. I'll say that for Dorothy, there wasn't any side to her. She always greeted the servants by their preferred name and even though normally she would be expected to call Verity by her surname, she never did. "A hunter is what I *ride*, not what I call my maid," I'd overheard her say, once.

If she was hungover, you would never have known. As usual, she was plastered in make-up and her hair hung in two precise curtains of smooth golden silk on either side of her face. Dorothy's looks reminded me a little of an illustration I'd seen once in an old story book of Snow White, that of the wicked queen. Beautiful but a little bit frightening too. But then, appearances could be deceptive. Dorothy was mostly kind, if a little bit careless, and, like I said before, never made you feel the vast gap that yawned between 'them' and 'us'.

"God, my head," she groaned, flinging herself down on the bed and reaching for her onyx and silver cigarette case. "I'm going to have to tell Dickie not to let me near the champagne cocktails again. I can't be trusted." She lit her cigarette and tossed the lighter onto her bedside table. "Was that my brother doing all the shouting just now?"

"Afraid so," said Verity. "He and your mother were having a bit of a row about money."

Dorothy laughed cynically. "So what's new? He's such a bore. You know, he has a perfectly adequate allowance?" Of course, we didn't know this, or I didn't, though I didn't confess my ignorance. Dorothy went on. "I mean, if I can't get through it in a month, I can't believe Peter can. What's he spending it on? I simply can't imagine."

I couldn't imagine it either. Imagine having that much money that you couldn't spend it all in a month, despite all the cocktails, cigarettes, new dresses, handbags and trips to the theatre that you paid for. For a moment, I had to struggle not to let my envy show on my face.

I had to get back to the kitchen, anyway, so I murmured to Verity that I would see her later, bobbed a little curtsey to Dorothy and hurried back down the stairs.

The full family contingent sat down to dinner that night. One of the parlourmaids, Nora, was ill and in bed with a bad stomach, so it fell to me to wait the table. Not something I enjoyed – I was always sure I was going to spill something hot onto someone, or let the potatoes bounce off the serving platter and all over the floor. I remembered Verity telling me once about how she'd seen one of the parlourmaids in her previous place spill a load of hot peas down the cleavage of one of the guests, and then have the excruciating task of trying to help the screaming guest retrieve them. It had made me laugh a lot at the time, but now I cursed the memory and prayed that my hands wouldn't shake and do anything like that.

As it turned out, it was fine. I handed the last dish of vegetables around and then stepped back to my place in the corner of the room, next to Mr Fenwick, the butler. It was quite dark in the room. The ground floor and first floor of the house were wired for electricity and there were adequate wall lights in the dining room, but Lady Eveline always demanded candlelight for the dinner table. "Wonderfully flattering for the complexion, candlelight," Dorothy had said once and that was probably why her Ladyship insisted on that particular form of light. I felt pleasantly invisible over in my dim corner. If it wasn't for the ache in my feet, I would have felt quite content.

I watched Lord Cartwright as he ate. He always cut his meat as if attacking it, with short jabs of his knife and fork, and swilled it down with wine. If he hadn't been quite so wealthy and titled, I had the suspicion that at least some of the guests who'd eaten here on occasion might have thought him just a little bit uncouth. He wasn't an attractive man – with his drooping moustache and ruddy complexion, he reminded me of nothing so much as a sunburnt walrus.

I found the trick to observing someone was to watch them for just long enough, but no longer. Stare intently at someone for too long, and, sooner or later, they look up and catch your eye. Try it, I assure you it's true. So I watched Lord Cartwright for just long enough and then swapped my gaze to his wife. True to her class, she was barely touching her food, pushing it disinterestedly around the plate. I knew full well that she'd have a tray sent up later – I imagined that she'd absolutely gorge herself then, eating with both hands, with no dining etiquette to stop her. The sight of Lady Cartwright rejecting my lovingly made food began to anger me so I looked further down the table to where Peter Drew was eating, in a sort of stiff, unhappy way. He didn't look like a man who was enjoying himself. Dorothy was seated next to him but she wasn't eating either, just resting her sleek head on one hand, a cigarette held unlit in her long fingers. I couldn't imagine either Lord or Lady Cartwright allowing her to actually smoke at the table. In that, I agreed with them.

Duncan Cartwright and Rosalind Makepeace were seated next to one another but weren't talking. It may have been my fancy, but they seemed to be slightly turned away from one another, as if they were holding the side of their bodies closest to the other stiff. It made me remember that time I'd had to sit at the servants' table at the position I'd had before Asharton – I'd had to sit next to the valet, who was a horrible man, and every dinner time it was the same; I hadn't been able to let the side next to him relax at all.

I'd noticed that before, the slight tension that always seemed to be between Rosalind and Duncan. I made a mental note to ask Verity why she thought that was and then pulled myself together with a jump as I realised they'd finished their main course, and I was now expected to help the footmen clear the table.

After dinner came the inevitable washing up and the preparation of breakfast for tomorrow. At least Maggie, the scullery maid, was the one who had to do most of the scrubbing. Mrs Watling and I sat at the table to go through the supplies and plans for what we had to do tomorrow.

Verity came in after a few minutes, yawning. "Can I make up a milky drink, Mrs Watling?"

"Of course, love. Is it for Dorothy?"

Verity nodded, sitting down at the table. "She's having an early night tonight, thank the Lord. I'm just about ready to drop."

"Miss Dorothy won't be wanting anything else to eat?"

Verity shook her head. "No, I wouldn't have thought so."

As she spoke, we could see one of the bells start jangling. "That'll be Madam," said Mrs Watling with a sigh. "She'll be wanting her tray."

"I'll take it up," I offered. I could see Lady Cartwright was in the library by the name on the bouncing bell, and I never missed an opportunity to visit the library. I love books. I love reading and writing, even if I barely get the chance to do either. The library at Merisham Lodge was large and square and filled with literally hundreds of books. I might even have a chance to sneak myself a new novel to read if I was sly about it.

"Good girl. Well, Joan, once you've taken that tray up you can turn in for the night. There's nothing more to do here."

Verity made the hot milk drink, yawning all the while, and carried it out the door, flapping a vague hand at me in goodbye. I went through to the pantry where the tray for Lady Cartwright was neatly laid out, covered in a white cloth, and picked it up with a grunt. At least the library was on the ground floor of the lodge, only one flight of stairs to climb.

There was no answer to my careful knock at the library door. I hesitated, knocked again and when there was silence, opened the door, picked up the tray from where I'd put it down on the floor, and edged inside.

27

I thought for a moment that the room was empty, but a second glance showed me Lady Cartwright over by the window, staring out at the dark garden. I could see her face reflected in the glass of the window and she looked deep in thought, almost, one might say, worried. Fearful, even? But of what?

"Your tray, Madam," I murmured.

She seemed to come back to life then and turned. "Oh, yes," she said, disinterestedly. "Put it there."

I placed the tray on the table she'd indicated and straightened up. I knew a 'thank you' would not be forthcoming. "Will that be all, Madam?"

She didn't bother to answer. She'd turned back to stare out of the window again, almost as though I wasn't there at all. I thought about asking her whether she wanted me to draw the curtains, but decided against it. Instead, I bobbed a curtesy and saw myself out, thoughts of stealing a book forgotten.

Verity was fast asleep by the time I got back to our room. I sighed, a bit disappointed that we wouldn't be able to chat. Instead, I fetched some clean water for the wash bowl on the stand, washed my face, cleaned my teeth and began the slow, laborious work of unpinning my hair. Verity had left the oil lamp burning, which she always did if I was going to be later than her. I could feel my eyelids drooping and knew I should just curl up under the blankets and let myself sleep, but part of me was cross that this was the only time I ever really got to myself and almost all of it was spent unconscious. I picked up my notebook and pen and started to write, continuing a story idea that I'd had while clearing up the kitchen that evening. I nurtured dreams of being a real writer, of seeing my own words in print. That was one thing I'd never confessed to anybody, not even Verity. That was the one dream I couldn't bear to have stamped on or laughed at. Not that Verity would do either of those things, but still... It was no use, that night. I couldn't keep my eyelids from fluttering closed. Giving in, I tucked the notebook and pen under my bed and turned off the lamp.

Chapter Three

I WAS UP BRIGHT AND EARLY the next morning, feeling well rested for a change. My first task of the day in the kitchen was always to make a start on the breakfasts, and I set to with a will, chopping mushrooms, breaking eggs and peeling damp slices of bacon from the greaseproof packet the butcher had delivered yesterday. Maggie had just finished mopping the kitchen floor and I had to tread carefully on the wet tiles to avoid slipping.

Once everything was underway, I filled the kettle and put it on the hob. Mrs Watling liked a good, hot cup of tea first thing when she came through to the kitchen, and after my hard work of the last half an hour I was ready for one too. As I lit the gas, a sound at the edge of hearing made me catch my breath. Was that – was that a scream? I stood still for a moment, straining my ears, but there was nothing, no other sound like the one I'd so briefly heard. Or had I? Shrugging mentally, I turned to get the cups from the dresser, laid them out and poured out the tea.

Something flickered in the corner of my vision and I turned, expecting to see Mrs Watling in the doorway. It wasn't her. It was Verity.

One glance told me something was terribly wrong.

"V? Verity? What's wrong?"

Verity didn't answer. She was chalk white, milk white, so pale that for a second she looked like a ghost of herself in the gloom. She was swaying very slightly.

"Verity?" I asked, now thoroughly alarmed. Quickly, I moved over to her. "What's wrong?"

She looked at me then and I grew even more anxious. Her eyes were huge, horrified pools.

I could see Verity trying to speak but nothing came from her dry mouth. "Over here," I said, and almost dragged her over to one of the kitchen chairs. She flopped into it as if all the strength had left her legs, and I quickly fetched her a glass of water.

She took a sip, and then another, the water splashing over the sides as her hand shook. Then she looked up at me. "She's dead," she whispered.

I had a sudden, shocking memory of that time in Asharton Manor, seeing Violet the housemaid run into the kitchen there, gibbering with fear. *It's Madam, it's Madam – she's lying there all cold, there's something wrong – all* cold *– I think she's dead...*

I swallowed down the bubble of nausea that had risen in my throat. "V? Verity? Who's dead?"

Verity put the glass back on the table, having spilt most of the water. "Lady Eveline."

I gasped. "What do you mean?"

"Lady Eveline. I went into the library to fetch Lord Cartwright's spectacles and – and—" Her voice started to tremble. "And she's lying there on the carpet, dead."

Her gaze rose to meet mine, her eyes dark and horrified. For a moment, shock overwhelmed me and I couldn't think of a thing to say.

Eventually I regained the power of speech. "Do you think she had a fit or something?"

Verity shook her head. "It's worse than that. Much worse than that."

I went cold. "What do you mean?"

Verity said nothing for a moment. She got up from the table, moving like an old woman. "Can you come with me? I need to show you."

I didn't respond straight away. I looked towards the stove, where the half-prepared breakfasts were waiting. Then I sighed. "Of course. Of course I'll come with you."

The two of us ran up the stairs to the hallway and raced down the corridor towards the library. We didn't meet anyone else on the way, and as we passed the staircase, I cocked an ear for sounds of the household getting up. It must have still been too early, for I could hear nothing.

Verity paused outside the library door. She was shaking, and I wasn't much better myself.

"Oh God, I don't think I can do it, I don't think I can look at her again," Verity whispered. She looked at me in anguish and then gulped and opened the door.

It was dark in the library, close and stuffy, and the usual smells of musty old books, old cigarette smoke and wood-smoke were undercut by something else, something sharp and coppery and dangerous. *Blood*, I told myself, holding my arms across my body to stop myself shivering. Fearfully, I looked where Verity was pointing.

At first I didn't think it was too bad, as I only saw her feet to start with. Lady Eveline was lying by her desk, crumpled onto her side, one arm out flung on the Persian rug beneath her. It was dim in the library, only one curtain pulled back at the window, and I stepped forward to see a bit better. That was when I saw her head, and the damage that had been done to it, and I screamed despite myself.

"Don't! Don't, Joan." Verity clutched my arm.

"I'm sorry," I said, gasping. "It was just the shock."

Lady Eveline had been bludgeoned to death. I tore my eyes away from the blood and looked at the patterns on the carpet, trying to force the image from my head. I looked until the swirls of the pattern began to echo inside my head.

"Joanie—"

I came to with a start. Verity was shaking me gently.

"Joanie, keep yourself together. I don't want you to faint."

"I won't faint," I muttered. Trying to breathe deeply, I pulled myself upright. "We have to tell someone straight away."

Verity nodded, her eyes huge. "Shouldn't the police be informed?"

"That's not our job." I thought of who we should tell. Mr Fenwick, the butler, or Mrs Anstells, the housekeeper.

"I suppose it should be Mr Fenwick," Verity whispered, reading my mind.

"Come on, then." I grabbed her hand and pulled her towards the door, desperate to get out of that blood-soaked room.

We flew down the corridor and down the stairs to where Mr Fenwick had his butler's pantry. I had only ever been in there once, to receive a ponderous message of approval for a dinner party for which Mrs Watling and I had worked like slaves. Mr Fenwick seemed old to me, even for a head butler.

He opened the door to our hurried, loud knocks

with disapproval already knitting his tufty white eyebrows.

"What is the meaning of this? Verity? I'm surprised at you."

We fell over ourselves to explain, talking over one another.

"It's Madam—"

"She's been killed, she's lying there dead in the library—"

"Mr Fenwick, you have to help—"

It took some time before we could make ourselves plain. Almost as white as his eyebrows, Mr Fenwick ordered us to remain where we were and marched out of the room.

Murder has its own rhythm. I knew that, after what I'd been through at Asharton Manor. Within twenty minutes of Mr Fenwick discovering that we'd been telling the truth about Lady Eveline, the whole house was in uproar. Verity had to go upstairs to tend to Dorothy, who'd apparently fainted when she was told of her mother's death. Mrs Watling and I attempted to get some sort of breakfast together but we might as well have not bothered – nobody was eating a thing. I collected the untouched dishes from the dining room, gone stone cold, and was walking back through the hallway to the kitchen stairs when I saw something through the front windows that made me freeze. Three black cars approached the house and as they got closer, tyres crunching over the gravel, I could see the 'Police' signs on the car roofs of all three. They hadn't wasted much time, I thought and then jumped as the doorbell rang. Hurriedly, china chinking on the tray, I went downstairs again. As I put the loaded tray on the kitchen table, I could hear Mr Fenwick's footsteps, approaching the front door up above, somewhat faster than his normal, stately tread.

It was a strange day. Verity hurried down the stairs to the kitchen about three hours after she'd first gone up to Miss Dorothy.

"Have we got any brandy?" she asked in a rush.

"Yes," I said, reaching for the bottle. "Want to put some in Dorothy's coffee, is that it?"

"I don't know what else to do." Verity sounded close to tears. "She's hysterical. She keeps screaming and crying and yelling. I thought if she could just get some sleep..."

She was very pale herself, and there were large dark circles under her eyes.

"Have you eaten anything today?" I asked sharply.

Verity shook her head.

"Right," Mrs Watling said, taking charge. She took the silver breakfast tray from Verity's shaking hands and put it on the table. "Sit down here." She almost shoved Verity into a sitting position. I slid a plate of bacon and bread in front of her.

"Mrs Watling's right," I said. "If you don't eat something you'll faint, and then you'll be no good to Dorothy at all."

"That's true." Verity fell on the food ravenously. I put a mug of tea down in front of her as well, and Mrs Watling followed it up with a small glass filled with the cooking sherry.

"Get that down you, too, Verity," she said firmly. "We've all a long day ahead of us."

I watched Verity eating, wishing I could be more help to her, but what could I do? My duties lay down here. I turned back to the stove-top and began stirring the soup, listening to the thump of policemen's feet up above my head.

Chapter Four

THE DAY WENT ON, SUPERFICIALLY, as normal. Mrs Watling and I prepared the meals, made up the menus for the following day, and marked up the order sheets for the grocer. Maggie and I scrubbed and polished and chopped as usual. While overhead, all we could hear all morning was the heavier tread of the police as they walked back and forth, from room to room. At about half past eleven, I heard the noise of an engine, noisier than a normal car would have been, and realised that the mortuary van had arrived. It was funny but I'd been getting on with things quite well up to that point, almost as though someone else was controlling my hands and my thoughts. I felt oddly detached from myself – even when I burnt myself on one of the pots on the hob. I barely registered the pain. I suppose I was still in shock. Sadly, unlike Dorothy, I couldn't fall about in hysterics and demand brandy and scream the place down. No, not me. I just had to get on with it, so I did, feeling all the while as if I'd been breathing in the fumes of something poisonous, something that made me feel dazed and sleepy but still somehow able to function.

The noise of the mortuary van broke through all that. I'd been cutting cold roast beef – Mrs Watling had decided on a cold lunch, why bother cooking something hot when nobody was going to eat it, she'd said, and I agreed – and until I heard the low, throaty roar of the engine outside in the yard, the fact that I was carving moist, pinkish meat hadn't bothered me. Now, I looked down at my hand with the knife and the reddish stain the meat had left on the chopping board and suddenly, I was back there in the library with Verity this morning, looking at Lady Eveline lying on the carpet.

I just about made it to the privy in time. What little breakfast I had eaten came up and I hung over the bowl, my trembling hands braced against the wall, feeling as weak and ill as if I really had been poisoned. After a moment, I managed to pull myself together enough to wipe my mouth and reach up to pull the flush.

"Joan?" Mrs Watling's voice called from the other side of the door. "Are you all right?" She must have seen my lightning dash from the kitchen.

"I'm fine," I said after a moment, my feeble voice betraying me. I straightened up gingerly and took a few deep breaths before unlatching the door.

"You're as white as a sheet," Mrs Watling half-scolded. She almost carried me back to the kitchen and installed me in a chair. "If I give you a little drop of cooking sherry are you going to be able to keep it down?"

I rubbed my sweating forehead. "I'll try."

She poured it out for me, and I sipped it gingerly. It warmed me all the way down and I sighed with something like relief.

"Now, just sit there for a moment—" Mrs Watling said just as a uniformed officer and two men in suits came into the kitchen. The two of us looked at them in alarm.

"Sorry to disturb you ladies," said the older man, quite a dapper gent in his black suit and close-cut beard. "I'm Detective Inspector Marks of Scotland Yard. This is Detective Sergeant Willis and Constable Crewe. May I ask which of you is Joan Hart?"

I swallowed and sat up a little straighter. "That's me, sir."

"I see." Detective Inspector Marks gave me quite a kindly smile. "Now, don't be alarmed, Miss Hart, but we just need to see you for a few moments. You're not in any trouble."

I didn't see how I could be so I wasn't particularly alarmed. Mrs Watling looked very anxious, almost as if she thought they were going to arrest me there and then. It was as much to get that look off her face as it was for my own curiousity that I gathered my courage and asked a question. "Is this because I was one of the people to discover the body of her ladyship, sir?"

Detective Inspector Marks looked a little surprised at my asking. The look he gave me was slightly more respectful than any he had given me before. "That's exactly right, Miss Hart. Would you come this way?"

I looked across at Mrs Watling, tacitly asking for her permission. She nodded, looking a little less worried than before.

The police officers took me up the stairs, across the hallway, and into the smaller of the two drawing rooms. Even though they'd only been here a matter of hours, they'd already taken over the place. The main table had been cleared of the flowers that Verity arranged so well and papers and pens were scattered over its glossy surface, along with a tea-tray of dirty cups and saucers. There were also two ashtrays, full to brimming already.

"Please sit down." Inspector Marks indicated a vacant chair, and I did as I was told. I folded my hands in my lap in the approved fashion and waited.

"Now, Miss Hart, we've talked to your fellow maid, Miss Verity Hunter, who I understand was the first person to discover the body of Lady Eveline. Can you tell me what happened this morning when she came to tell you? In your own words and taking your time."

I composed myself for a moment before answering. Then I went back over the sequence of events as best I could remember. The inspector listened intently and scribbled in his notebook. I was surprised when I saw it. It was just one of the cheap red ones that I bought myself, the cheapest possible notebook you could buy. I suppose the police have to keep their costs down, as much as anyone else does, but it seemed incongruous that all the words I spoke on so grave a subject would be entered into a thin little two-penny booklet. I suppose if I'd imagined it at all, I would have thought the inspector would write in something large, impressive and covered in expensive black leather.

I think I spoke quite well. It was only when I got to the bit where Verity and I had first seen the body that my voice faltered, and I had to stop to swallow down the bubble of nausea that rose in my throat.

Inspector Marks was watching me keenly. "Would you like a glass of water, Miss Hart?"

I took a few deep breaths and felt better. "No, thank you, sir. I'm quite all right, now."

"Very well." The inspector put down his pen and cheap notebook and favoured me with another kindly smile. "Now, you've given us a very thorough account of yours and Miss Hunter's movements this

42

morning, so I'm grateful for that." I bobbed my head in a kind of sitting down curtsey, not exactly sure whether I was being dismissed or not. The inspector hesitated for a moment, as if weighing something up. "I wonder, could you tell me how long you've worked for the family?"

"Not very long. I was in service in Kilburn, in London, before I came here about three months ago."

"Perhaps you could let Constable Crewe here have the particulars of your previous position when you have a moment?" It was an order, not a request. I said nothing but nodded my head again.

There was a longer silence while the inspector made another note in his notebook. I was on the verge of asking whether I could be dismissed when he looked up again. His next words took me by surprise.

"You seem an intelligent young woman," Inspector Marks said. I wondered if I was the only one to hear the unspoken sentence that followed his words. *For your class.* "Do you have any ideas at all as to whether Lady Eveline had any enemies?"

It was as if Verity had suddenly leapt into my head and taken control of my tongue. I heard myself say "Well, she must have had *one*, mustn't she, sir?"

I heard someone, either the sergeant or the constable suppress a snort of amusement. The inspector's eyes narrowed.

Hurriedly, I went on. "I'm sorry, sir, I didn't mean to be impertinent. It was just that the question took me a little by surprise."

I bit my lip, expecting a sharp word from the inspector, or worse. Somehow, Verity could get away with saying things like that, every time. It probably helped that she managed to say them with a twinkle in her eye. With me, it just came out sounding rude.

"Well, you're correct in that assumption," the inspector said rather drily, after a moment. I sagged with relief, inwardly. "But is there anything else you can tell me that might be useful?" I was frantically thinking back over things when he added, "There's been some reports about an argument Lady Eveline had with her son, Peter Drew, yesterday."

"Oh, yes," I said, relieved, because that had just occurred to me, and I hadn't been sure whether it was my place to mention it or not. I didn't know Peter Drew from Adam, really, but I wouldn't want to get an innocent man into trouble. "Yes, I'm afraid I did overhear some sharp words between them. Both Verity and I did," I added hurriedly, afraid that it sounded as though I'd been listening at doors.

"What was it that was said?"

I thought for a moment, trying to remember. "Her ladyship said something about not wanting to bail him out again. I think that was it. And he said—" I stopped for a moment, remembering Peter's words. "He said something about how people might be interested to hear one or two things about her."

The inspector's pen was poised. "About Lady Eveline?" he prompted.

"I suppose so, sir. I'm sorry but that's all I can remember." I could feel my hands twisting around each other in my lap. I wanted to ask if Peter Drew was a suspect, but I didn't quite dare.

I was dismissed after that with a casual thank you. I got up, bobbing a vague curtsey. It's quite hard to curtsey to three corners of the room at once. Then I walked to the door, forcing myself not to scurry.

Outside, the hallway was empty. I hesitated and did something that surprised myself. I held my breath and leant back, in towards the closed door, listening.

You develop a fine ear, when you're a servant. It's funny how often the gentry think that if they murmur something – some scandal or some complaint – it won't be overheard. I could hear the inspector's deep voice quite clearly through the wood.

"Interesting that that's the third report of the row between the mother and son," he said.

"Think she could have told us more?" That had to be Sergeant Willis.

"Perhaps." I could hear the scrape of the chair legs against the floor as the inspector got up. "You have to tread carefully with these girls. They're apt to get hysterical if you push them too hard."

"That one seems steady enough." Sergeant Willis again.

"Yes, capable young woman, I would have thought—"

Before I could hear anything else, the front doorbell rang, shattering the silence. I jumped about a foot in the air. When my feet connected with the floor again, I ran as quickly and as quietly towards the kitchens as I could, before Mr Fenwick could arrive and catch me eavesdropping.

Chapter Five

IT SEEMED AN ENDLESS DAY. At ten o'clock, I put the last wiped and shining pan away in the cupboard and closed it wearily. Mrs Watling had long since gone to her own room. I untied my dirty apron and bundled it in my arms, ready to carry it upstairs.

The floors above were finally silent. There was still a police officer here, Constable Crewe, stationed in the drawing room and obviously here for the night. I'd taken him up a tray of sandwiches and coffee at nine, and he'd thanked me with real gratitude. He wasn't a handsome man, having rather too much chin, and I could never abide a man with hairy hands. I could see the other maids didn't share my feelings. They'd fluttered and twittered around him like a flock of silly birds and kept making excuses to take more wood and coal in for the drawing room fire, so much that you'd think it would keep burning until Christmas without being replenished. Perhaps it was the uniform.

All these thoughts went around and around my

tired head as I climbed the servants' stairs. It was good, in a way; it stopped me thinking about the library, the blood on the carpet, and the state of Lady Eveline when Verity and I had found her. Even so, flashes kept coming back to me, like something from a bad dream, except one from which I was unable to wake.

I was the first one back in our room, unusually. I wondered what was keeping Verity. I knew she'd eventually managed to get Dorothy to take a sleeping tablet, so it couldn't be her mistress who was keeping her up. Or was it? Perhaps she'd had to talk to the police again. Oh, everything was in such a muddle, such confusion. I found myself wondering, rather incongruously, whether the murderer had realised what trouble they would cause when they decided to do what they did.

I sat down before our little mirror and began to unpin my hair, massaging the ache from my head as I did so. My face, reflected in the glass, looked pale and worried. Well, I *was* worried. For the first time, it occurred to me that I was living in a house with a murderer. The thought gave me a nasty prickle of fear, and I was getting up to lock the door when it opened and Verity walked in, almost dead on her feet.

She said nothing but cast herself full length on her creaking bed, burying her face in the pillow.

"V?" I asked tentatively after a moment.

"I never, ever want to live through another day like this ever again," came her muffled voice.

"Well, let's hope to God we never have to." I sat down next to her prone figure and patted her back. "Come on, you can't go to sleep in your clothes."

Verity groaned and heaved herself upright. "I know. I know. God, I'm tired."

We both began to undress, pulling our clothes off with fingers so clumsy with fatigue that the buttons and hooks resisted. Verity cursed freely, and I felt very much like doing so myself.

Eventually, tucked up in our respective beds, Verity leant forward to turn off the lamp. I remembered Asharton Manor, where I hadn't even had an oil lamp to read by but had to use candles, as if I were back in Victorian times. That was something to be thankful for, anyway. A memory of Dorothy's bedroom, with her silk-shaded bedside light and electric light bulb occurred to me with a jab of envy, but I quickly dismissed the thought. I had other things on my mind.

I put out a hand to stop her. "Wait. Wait a moment."

She looked at me with crooked eyebrows. "I'm absolutely all in, Joanie. Can't we sleep?"

"Yes – it's just—" I wasn't sure exactly what I wanted to say. "What did the police ask you?"

"Oh, you know, how I came to be in the library, what I saw—" Verity stopped and swallowed.

49

"Whether her ladyship had any enemies. Had I seen anyone strange around lately."

"Really?" They hadn't asked me that. Did the police think that the killer had been a stranger, someone from outside the house? At first the thought was a relief but, on reflection, I thought again. The idea of some murderous madman roaming the grounds of Merisham Lodge was almost as bad as thinking that the killer was someone we knew. I got up and checked that the door was locked. At least the door *had* a lock – it was because we were female and therefore vulnerable. The male servants' rooms didn't have a lock at all.

Verity's eyelids were drooping. "I had to tell them about the row Peter had with Lady E," she said, drowsily. "They asked me about it so I had to tell them. Didn't I?"

"Yes, of course." I took pity on her. "Come on, turn off the lamp and get some rest."

I think Verity was asleep before her head hit the pillow. I was deathly tired but somehow I just couldn't sleep. My head was a jumble of images and thoughts, none of them conducive to relaxation. Eventually exhaustion overcame me and a black curtain fell.

THE POLICE CAME BACK FIRST thing the next morning. It wasn't until I realised I was holding my breath, at the crunch of tires on the gravel, that I understood I'd been waiting for them to arrive ever since I woke up.

I forgot the bread I was making. I forgot everything. Instead, I found myself walking towards the door and towards the stairs.

"Wait. Joan—" Mrs Watling looked as though she was going to call me back. We exchanged a glance, and she must have seen something in my face because she shut her mouth abruptly. Then she nodded, tensely.

I turned and ran for the stairs.

I'd reached the back of the hallway when I heard the scream. It came from up the stairs, on the first floor of the house. It made me jump and hurry forward and then I realised it was Dorothy. She was up on the landing, half collapsed in Verity's arms. I saw Verity's face, white and shocked, and realised what was happening. The police had Peter Drew in handcuffs.

"No, no, no!" Dorothy kept screaming. I could see Verity struggling to keep her upright. For a moment, I stood still, unable to work out what to do to help. I couldn't go up the stairs – the police and Peter were coming down the staircase. Peter looked ill; his face set. The officers on either side of him I didn't recognise. Behind the three of them, walked Detective Inspector Marks and Sergeant Willis, their faces grim and forbidding.

They walked past me without a glance and headed for the door. I looked at Peter's hands, held in front of him as he walked past. The cuffs looked very heavy. Biting my lip, scarcely able to think over the noise that Dorothy was making, I watched the huge front door shut behind them.

"It's not true!" Dorothy was almost slumped on the floor by now. Making up my mind, I hurried up the stairs to Verity. A few of the servants were standing a few feet away, staring and whispering.

"Help me get her to her room," Verity gasped. Between the two of us, we managed to get Dorothy to her feet and virtually carried her along the corridor to her bedroom.

I fear we dumped her rather roughly on the white satin quilt but for someone so slender, she was awfully heavy. Verity drew the counterpane up to Dorothy's chin.

"Just rest, my lady," I heard her whisper. Dorothy sobbed and gulped.

Verity looked at me. "We'd better get her a drink," she murmured, pulling at my arm to lead me from the bedroom.

Hastening down the corridor together, I almost felt like crying myself. Everything seemed so chaotic; I wasn't sure what to think. Had Peter Drew killed his mother? It was a horrible thought.

Mrs Watling was at the stove when we reached

the kitchen, stirring something with feverish energy. She whirled around as soon as we arrived.

"Tell me it's not true," she said. There was pleading in her voice.

Verity sat down at the table as if all the strength had suddenly run out of her legs. "They've arrested Peter for the murder of her ladyship," she said flatly.

"That can't be true," Mrs Watling said. She sounded near tears. "It must be some mistake."

"I don't know what to think," said Verity. "Dorothy's in a dreadful state. I need to get her a brandy or something."

"Well – run along and ask Mr Fenwick if you can use the drinks cupboard." Mrs Watling turned back to the pot on the stove and stabbed at its steaming contents with the wooden spoon in her hand. "We'll all need a stiff drink by the end of the day and no mistake. My goodness, it feels as if I'm living in a nightmare. Master Peter, arrested for murder? I can't believe it."

I said nothing but silently tied my apron strings more tightly around my waist – they'd slipped loose as we'd carted Dorothy to her room. Verity sighed, got to her feet and squeezed my arm in farewell as she headed to wherever she could find Mr Fenwick.

I looked at the menu written up in chalk on the board over by the sink. Who could think about food at this time? It all seemed so meaningless. My hands automatically began to gather the utensils I needed but my brain was thinking of other things. Why had the police arrested Peter? On what evidence? Just on the fact that he'd had a quarrel with his mother the day before she was killed? From the sounds of it, that was quite usual whenever he turned up. Why had he killed her, if he *had* killed her? Because she wouldn't give him money?

It didn't sound very likely to me. I began chopping onions, blinking my eyes against the harsh fumes. Running my wrists under cold water sometimes worked to take the sting away, but not today. I dabbed my streaming eyes with my cuffs, glad of an excuse to have reddened eyelids. Perhaps it wasn't so unusual, but I felt rather like having a good cry and longed for the end of the day when I could hide my head under the blankets and sob.

I heard footsteps behind me and turned to see Verity coming back into the room. Her face looked as tired as I could feel mine to be.

"Mrs Watling, Joanie, I'm so sorry to be a bother but could you make up a tray for Dorothy? She's not really eaten anything since it happened, and I'm worried she's going to faint." Verity pinched the bridge of her nose as she spoke, screwing up her eyes. "I shouldn't have taken her the brandy. I can't keep her from pouring it down but at least I can try and soak some of it up."

"Of course," said Mrs Watling just as I nodded

in agreement. "Joan, scrambled eggs and a little bit of bacon, something like that. Lots of bread."

"And a strong pot of coffee," Verity said, slumping down at the table.

I put the onions to one side, thankfully, and turned to the stove to start assembling the tray. I was feeling impatient and annoyed with Dorothy but, as I slowly heated the pan for the eggs – it was important not to have too high a heat, as that was when the mixture would go rubbery – I realised I needed to be a bit more sympathetic. The poor girl had just lost her mother, after all, and in the most hideous way possible. And she'd lost her brother too, perhaps forever. Thinking back, I remembered her father had died some years ago. She was facing the loss of her whole family – I shouldn't be so hard on her.

I opened the oven door to turn the toast, thinking. On what evidence were the police holding Peter Drew? Surely not just that he'd had a quarrel with his mother the day before? I drew out the hot, crisp toast and slathered it with butter.

The tray arranged, the napkin folded, and the steaming coffee pot placed upon it, Wearily, Verity got up and went to take it.

"It's all right," I said quickly. "If Mrs Watling doesn't mind, I'll take it up for you." I shot a quick glance at the cook and she nodded her agreement. I felt a burst of gratitude for having such a sympathetic employer. She knew I was concerned about Verity.

"Thank you so much." Verity followed me out of the room as I bore the tray before me like a peace offering to place before a demanding god.

I hadn't seen Dorothy since Verity and I had deposited her weeping, shaking form on her bed that morning. Now, when we entered the room, she seemed scarcely aware of our presence. She sat in her satin dressing gown, in the middle of her rumpled bed, smoking and tapping the ash into an already brimming ashtray on the coverlet. The air in the room was blue with smoke and heady with the faint fumes from the empty brandy glass on the bedside table. The brandy bottle stood half-empty by its side. Dorothy stared into space, mechanically bringing the cigarette to her lips every other minute but otherwise doing nothing.

I heard Verity give a tiny sigh. I put the tray on a free portion of the bed. I wondered whether it would be rude to give my condolences or whether it would be more impertinent to speak at all.

As I put the tray down, Dorothy seemed to come back to life a little. Her dull gaze flickered and her red-rimmed eyes met mine.

"Oh, Joan," was all she said, very faintly.

"I'm so very sorry, my lady," I said on impulse, and for some reason tears came into my eyes. Her own filled in sympathy and her lips moved but I couldn't hear what she said. I think it was 'thank you'.

Verity bustled about, opening the window to let in some fresh air, taking the full ashtray away and replacing it with a clean one. She offered the plate of scrambled eggs, bacon and tomatoes to Dorothy, who cringed back as if it were a plate of horse dung.

"Please, my lady. You must eat something to keep your strength up," Verity pleaded. Dorothy said nothing but shook her head. Verity looked at me in despair but what could I do? I had less authority than Verity herself.

The door to the bedroom slammed back at that instant and Lord Cartwright strode in. He was so big and so unexpected that all three of us jumped. Verity had been standing nearest the door and if she hadn't quickly leapt out of the way, he would have knocked her over. As I saw her stumble back against the wall, I was conscious of a fierce surge of anger. We could have been invisible to him, that was the thing. We cleaned his house, cooked his food, made up his bed, emptied his chamber pots and did absolutely everything to ensure his life was one of ease and comfort, and what thanks did we get? Absolutely bugger all, as Verity would say. He treated us not as if we were the lowest of the low but as if we didn't exist in the first place. We weren't lowly to him, we just weren't even people at all.

Verity and I might as well have not been in the room. Lord Cartwright turned to his step-daughter with a look of anger and impatience. "Come on, get up," he said brusquely. "The police want to talk to you."

I felt a jump of unease at his words, but they didn't seem to bother Dorothy. She gave him a slow, contemptuous look and then pulled the breakfast tray onto her lap.

"I am having my breakfast," she said in a bored voice, after a moment.

"They aren't going to wait around forever."

"I will go down when I've finished my breakfast," Dorothy said, still in the same bored tone, and began to shovel the food into her face.

Lord Cartwright's ruddy face reddened further. "Don't make me drag you out of there, girl," he said in a tone that terrified me. I hadn't ever seen him this angry before. His gaze fell on Verity and she clearly snapped back into existence for him. He pointed a finger at her. "You! Make sure she's up and dressed in the next five minutes. Don't make me have to tell you twice."

Verity bobbed a tiny curtsey, her face set in the neutral expression every good servant learns to wear. That expression masked a lot. Outwardly, the face says 'of course, sir', but inwardly boils a sea of rage and hate. Lord Cartwright was getting the cursing of his life inside Verity's head, if he only knew it.

He slammed the door behind him as he went, and the curtains at the window billowed and eddied in the breeze created.

"My lady—" Verity began, but Dorothy, swallowing the last mouthful of egg and toast, held up a hand to stop her.

"It's all right," she said, when she could speak. "I'm getting up. I know I can't really keep the police waiting – and I don't want Lord C to give you a pasting as well as me."

Verity looked a little embarrassed, but as soon as she had finished speaking, Dorothy was off in that blank state again, staring forward into nothing. I found myself wondering, for the first time, what her feelings were towards her stepfather. What had her feelings been for her *mother*? Lady Eveline hadn't been exactly lovable but perhaps a daughter always loves her mother, no matter what. I wouldn't know.

Dorothy clearly loved her brother though, despite her disparaging words towards him when he'd arrived at the house. I could only begin to guess at her state of mind, thinking of him in prison. Would he be in prison yet, though? Surely not. He'd be held at the police station, at least until he was charged. Was that right? I realised I didn't know nearly enough about the judicial system in my own country and resolved to find out more, if I could. If I ever got more than five minutes to myself to do something other than work.

It was time for me to leave so that Verity could dress her mistress. I went to pick up the tray, just as Verity said, "Please try not to worry, my lady. I'm sure that Mr Drew will be found innocent, he can't be anything other than that."

That snapped Dorothy out of her blank stare. I watched her eyes spark back to life just as her face contracted in misery. "I'm afraid that's not the case, Verity."

Forgetting my place, I cried out, "But there's no evidence against him, is there, my lady? They can't be holding him just because of a silly quarrel."

Dorothy's burning gaze came around to meet my own. I flinched at the intensity of her stare.

After a moment, she spoke, quite coolly. "Oh, don't you know? They found gloves, *his* gloves, in his room. Gloves stained with my mother's blood."

Aghast, I stared at her. She held my gaze for a moment and then looked away. Stuttering out an apology, something like that, I bent to pick up the tray. My lasting impression, as I left the silent room, was of the shock on Verity's face, mirroring my own.

Chapter Six

I SLEPT LIKE THE DEAD THAT night. When I came to in the morning, in the cold grey light before the dawn, I saw with sleepy surprise that Verity was already sitting up in bed. She hadn't lit the lamp, but was sitting with her knees drawn up to her chest, a shawl around her shoulders. She looked worried.

"Are you all right, V?" I asked, rubbing sleep from my eyes.

Verity bit her lip. "I'm—" she began and then obviously thought better of it. "Listen, Joanie, go back to sleep. It's not time to get up yet."

So why was she awake then? I tried to formulate the right question in my head but I was still too tired. Murmuring something, I turned back over in bed to face the wall and went back to sleep.

Later, at breakfast, I could see Verity was still thinking something over. She had such an expressive face; I could see why some of her relatives had become actors. As we ate our porridge and drank our tea, I remembered Lord Cartwright yesterday, nearly knocking her for six as he thundered into the room. What a *pig* that man was. I knew I should feel sorry for him – he'd just lost his wife, after all – but I found it difficult to find even one crumb of sympathy for him.

I found it darkly amusing to wonder what Lord C would say if he knew Verity's origins – that on one side of her family, she was actually higher born than he was. Verity's father had been a minor aristocrat and he'd eloped with her mother, an actress, earning himself the infinite opprobrium of his high-born family and ensuring that he was cut out of his father's will forever. It was a romantic story – I often thought it would make a good novel, not that I would ever write it for fear of hurting Verity's feelings – but it was a sad one too. Verity's father had killed himself eventually, worn down by shame, debt and failed honour. Verity's mother had been left virtually penniless. She raised Verity by herself until that fateful day she and Verity, who was then just eight years old, had visited Covent Garden market in London, just as Spanish flu was beginning to spread its evil tentacles through the population of the capital. Influenza carried Verity's mother off in a matter of days, which is how Verity ended up at the orphanage with me.

I don't believe I have ever been so thankful for fate that she and I ended up in beds next to one another in the dormitory and that we became friends. Sometimes I felt guilty for thinking that. My good fortune in having her for a friend was entirely dependent on the fact that she'd lost all her loved ones. If I could go back and change time, make it so that her father and mother survived, would I do it, knowing it would mean we'd never meet?

Stop being so fanciful. I scolded myself as I took my plates towards the scullery for Maggie to wash. *As if you haven't got enough to worry about in the here and now.*

Life below stairs seemed slightly more normal than it had been for the past couple of days. The police were still here, interviewing the family. I'd caught a glimpse of Duncan Cartwright sitting next to Dorothy in the morning room with his arm around her shoulders. He looked pale and shocked, and Dorothy was in tears again. It was the first time I'd ever seen Duncan do anything sympathetic for anyone. I wondered whether he was mourning his stepmother. He and Lady Eveline had always seemed to get on quite well.

As Mrs Watling and I began preparations for dinner, I found myself wondering anew who could have murdered her ladyship. From overhearing Mr Fenwick and Mrs Anstells, I knew the police had found that a window in the library had been forced on the night of the murder. Whilst not conclusive in itself – the murderer could have done that to cover his or her tracks – it did suggest that there was a possibility the killer could have come from outside the house. How much the family must have been hoping for that, I thought, pushing steak through the mincer. It was still difficult to look at raw meat without a shudder of nausea but I had to get over that. It was either get over it or have to look for another kind of job, and where on Earth would I go and what would I do? Cooking was all I was trained to do.

Verity was very quiet all day; not that I saw much of her. Dorothy had been interviewed again by the police, and not long after, Verity had seen her back to her room. She came marching down to the kitchen with a set face, asking for more strong coffee. I had the impression that Dorothy was back to drowning her sorrows. Not that I could exactly blame her, but it made me cross for Verity, who had to bear the brunt of Dorothy's inebriation and mess-making and deal with all the clothes ruined by slopped brandy and spilled cigarette ash.

It was bath night, that night, and as usual, the female servants took it in turns to use one of the two servants' bathrooms on the top floor. A hot bath should have been a luxury, but it was always icy in the bathroom, with no heating and no fire. Verity and I usually shared the bath water – not at once, but taking it in turns, one after the other – and we used to help each other wash our hair. It was such a fuss with very long hair; the soap always took an age to rinse out. Verity kept threatening to get hers bobbed but I knew I probably wouldn't have the nerve.

There was satisfaction to be had, it was true, tucked up in bed in clean nightgowns, comfortably conscious of being washed, powdered and smelling sweet for once. I kept sticking my nose down the front of my nightgown to enjoy my clean, soapy scent.

"Joanie, stop doing that, you look deranged." Verity sat at the dressing table, carefully pinning up her damp hair. She caught my eye in the little mirror, and grinned. I stuck my tongue out at her.

Verity finished her pin curls and wound a filmy chiffon scarf around her head. She drew her shawl a little more firmly about her shoulders. Once we'd broken eye contact, the smile dropped off her face and she was back to looking worried once more.

I sighed and put down my book. "V, what is it?"

Her eyes met mine again in the mirror. "What?"

"You're worried about something. What is it?"

Verity bit her lip. Then, getting up, she checked the door to the room was locked and then got into bed. She looked over at me, her bottom lip pinched beneath her teeth.

"All right," she said after a moment. "I am worried."

"What is it?"

"It's what Dorothy said to us yesterday."

"What about?"

"The gloves." Verity's eyes met mine, wide and shocked. "Remember? She said the police had taken Peter because they found his gloves, bloody gloves, in his room."

I winced. "Yes, I remember. Horrible."

Verity hugged her knees to her chest, looking like a little girl. "It's just this," she said. "I took some washing into Peter's room quite early in the morning before they arrested him."

There was clearly more, but she stopped speaking. "Go on," I prompted.

"Well," Verity said, hesitantly. "That was a few hours before they made the arrest, right? They must have searched his room that morning, after I'd been in there."

"And?"

Verity sighed. "Those gloves weren't there. They weren't there that morning."

I stared at her. "What do you mean?"

Verity became animated. "I asked Dorothy and she said the police found these bloody gloves stuffed at the back of a drawer, his underwear drawer, as it happened." She half smiled. "Well, I had to put some clothes away for him in that drawer, and I never saw any gloves there, bloody or otherwise."

I was silent for a moment, thinking. "Could he – could he have put them in there after you put the clothes away?"

Verity shook her head decisively. "No. He couldn't have, because he was with Dorothy that whole morning, right up until they came to arrest him."

She stopped speaking and we stared at one another.

"So," I said slowly, unwillingly. "So, that means that someone else must have put them there. Right?"

Verity was silent for a moment. "I can't think of another explanation that fits," she said. "I've been trying all day to see if I can think of another reason, but I can't."

I closed my eyes briefly. "Oh Lord, this is all we need."

Another silence fell. Selfishly, I wished for one moment that Verity hadn't told me. I *really* wished she hadn't told me just before bedtime. Now I would probably lie awake all night, worrying about it and what to do.

I looked over at Verity and saw the dark half-moons under her eyes. My momentary anger vanished. Now I realised why she'd been up so early. I felt bad then, that my good friend had fretted and worried while I slumbered beside her, no help at all.

"So what do we do?" I asked.

Verity bit her lip again. "I think the only thing to do is go to the police."

"Yes." I couldn't see any way around that. "And

V – one thing. Don't go mentioning this to anyone else, all right? It could be dangerous."

Verity half smiled. "I remember giving you much the same warning, once."

"Well, quite. And you were quite right to."

Verity yawned and slid down beneath her covers. "Don't worry, I'm not going to tell anyone except Inspector Marks. And now, I really must sleep, I'm ready to drop."

"Good night, then."

I sat there in the dim light, listening to Verity's breathing softening into sleep. Then I turned off the lamp, watching as darkness slid into the room. After a moment, I slid down in the bed, pulled the blankets up to my chin, and laid there, staring at nothing, looking into the night.

Chapter Seven

IT WAS ABSOLUTELY TYPICAL, AS things turned out. For three days, you couldn't throw a stick without hitting a policeman, and now that we actually *wanted* to talk to Inspector Marks, he was nowhere to be found. Verity sometimes ate breakfast in our room, particularly if Dorothy had had a late night the night before, but this morning she appeared in the kitchen and came up to me as I chopped mushrooms on one of the counters.

"I'm going to see if I can see the inspector today," she murmured, leaning in as if inspecting my chopping skills. I could tell she didn't want to be overheard.

"Want me to come with you?" I was wondering how I was going to manage that, given the lunch Mrs Watling and I had to prepare. It was Maggie the scullery maid's morning off and the washing up was piling up even as we spoke. As was usual, murder or no murder, the family was expecting the full five courses for dinner.

"If you could, Joanie, that would be wonderful." I saw her glance at the piles of vegetables by my elbow with disquiet. "If you can't get away though…"

"I'll try," I promised, and she was happy enough with that.

The morning rolled relentlessly towards lunchtime. Mrs Watling asked me to make clear soup for the starter, which was a fiddly job at the best of times. I said nothing but pushed a stray strand of hair off of my forehead and nodded. I couldn't stand it when the kitchen was in a mess like it was – it felt overwhelming, as if I'd never be able to finish anything. Mrs Watling must have caught the edge of my panic.

"Joan, don't worry. I'll have one of the boot boys finish the washing up. Just pile it all up in the sink and get on with the soup."

"Yes, Mrs Watling." I silently gnashed my teeth as I reached for the greaseproof paper. Of course, we *would* have run out. I said as much to Mrs Watling, hoping she'd say we could do something else for the starter instead. No such luck.

"There's more in the cupboard along from the study," Mrs Watling said absently, her attention concentrated on the butter and peppercorn sauce for the beef. "Just run up and grab another roll."

Fuming, I yanked at my apron strings and pulled it over my head. It was one thing to be covered in splashes and stains and grease-marks down in the kitchen but another when going 'up above'. I'd once overheard Lady Eveline speaking sharply to Mrs Anstells about the importance of "the maids always looking neat and respectable when they are above stairs." It would have made me laugh if I hadn't been so cross. How on Earth did her ladyship think the housemaids would be able to clean out the fires without getting covered in soot? Or the kitchen maids would be able to prepare all the food for the house without getting even a little bit dirty? Then I remembered the poor woman was dead, and guilt extinguished the flames of my anger.

I smoothed down the front of my dress, checked that my cuffs were fairly respectable, and climbed the stairs to the main hallway. The study lay off a corridor that ran behind the length of the drawing room. It wasn't an area I knew well. I found myself almost tiptoeing as I hurried along the carpet towards the cupboard. The door to the study was slightly ajar, and as I softly walked past it, I could hear the bass rumble of a male voice coming from the room.

Quietly, I opened the cupboard door and started looking for the greaseproof paper. There were boxes and bundles of all sorts of things in the cupboard, and I stood scanning the shelves, looking for the distinctive long cardboard box. I recognised the voice of the man in the study – it was Lord Cartwright himself. Not wanting to have him confront me – I wasn't doing anything wrong, but then, when had that ever stopped him? – I redoubled my search efforts, carefully moving aside boxes and bags and all the time trying to be as quiet as a mouse.

"You've been such a godsend throughout this awful time, my dear," I heard Lord Cartwright say. Surely he wasn't speaking to Dorothy in that gentle tone? Curious, despite myself, I found myself listening more closely.

A woman's voice replied. "I'm sure I do the very best I can, my lord." Who was that? After a moment, the penny dropped. Of course, it was Rosalind. She was Lord Cartwright's secretary, after all. It was perfectly natural that she would be working with him in the study. Despite that though, there was *something*… I found myself holding my breath, listening harder.

"A good girl, yes, a very good girl. And you know, my dear, that good girls will always be rewarded—" His lordship's voice sank a little and I couldn't hear any more. At the same time, I spotted the greaseproof paper box, right at the back of the cupboard. Grabbing it, I closed the door very quietly. That was when I should have left, I know. But I didn't. Instead, I crept as close to the study door as I could and listened.

There was silence from within the room, then a rustle. Was that a giggle I heard from Rosalind? I couldn't tell. Eyes wide, I inclined my head a little further towards the gap.

There was a creak of floorboards within the room and the sound of footsteps walking towards the door. I jumped, lost my head and instead of turning back down the corridor towards the kitchens, ran further along it to where a small alcove housed an ornament cabinet. I flattened myself against the side of it just as the door to the study opened fully. I could see quite clearly through the glassed-in side of the cabinet. Rosalind walked out of the study, carrying an armful of books and papers. Her hair was as neat and smooth as normal but her cheeks were stained pink. I stared, wondering exactly what it was I'd just overheard.

Once she'd disappeared around the corner, I snuck out from my hiding place, clutching my greaseproof paper, and hurried back along the corridor, my face burning.

I was quite pleased to have a job that demanded some concentration when I got back to the kitchen. Those few overheard words raced around and around in my head. Had I actually witnessed anything untoward or not? Was I imagining things? And did it signify anything if indeed I *had* witnessed some sign of affection between his lordship and his assistant? Mechanically, I whisked the soup with crushed egg-shells, skimming off the scum that formed on top until most of it was gone. The greaseproof paper was then used to clarify the soup until it reached the desired clear golden colour.

Maggie had returned, thank God, and she and the youngest boot boy, Norman, were busy at the sinks. The beef was resting and Mrs Watling had just brought the beautifully cooked vegetables out from the stove. Everything was back under control – in the kitchen, at least.

Lunch was served upstairs and then we all sat down to our more modest offering. Verity was nowhere to be seen. I wondered whether she was eating with Dorothy in her room – she did that sometimes, when Dorothy wanted company but didn't want to bother with the luncheon table downstairs. Had Verity had time to talk to the inspector yet? Having heard what I'd just heard, I wondered whether that was something I ought to mention as well. Then again, what hard evidence did I have that something was going on between Lord Cartwright and Rosalind Makepeace? Absolutely none, I told myself firmly, arranging my knife and fork neatly on my empty plate.

After lunch, Mrs Watling and I had a rare hour of relaxation before preparation for dinner got underway. Mrs Watling had a cup of tea and a doze in the armchair by the fire in the servants' hall. I decided I'd try and find Verity. I wanted to talk to her about whether she'd managed to relay her information about the gloves to the inspector – and whether she'd ever seen or heard anything untoward between his lordship and Rosalind.

I checked our room, Dorothy's room and all of the main rooms in the house. I made sure I carried a small stack of aprons and took care to bustle. *Always look as if you're going somewhere specific*, Verity had told me once. *Never be empty-handed. Then you always look as though you're meant to be wherever they might find you. It's the girls who lollygag about who get reprimanded.*

As it was, I saw none of the family and precious few of the other servants. The house could be like that sometimes – it was almost eerie, the way that it seemed to empty out at times. I wondered whether Verity had accompanied Dorothy out – but even I couldn't see Dorothy off shopping or partying just days after the brutal murder of her mother. I glanced at the grandfather clock in the hallway as I went past and saw that it was nearly time to go back to work. What a waste of a free hour...

Just as I was coming back into the kitchen, I almost cannoned into Verity in the doorway itself. The surprise made us both shriek.

"There you are," I exclaimed. "I've been looking all over for you."

Verity grabbed my arm and drew me back into the kitchen. "I've just spotted the inspector, he's out in the garden. I'm going to see him now."

"Oh, right out in the open?" I felt a qualm. "Are you sure that's wise, V?"

"I might not get another chance. Dorothy's asleep at the moment but she won't be for long. Are you coming?"

I glanced at the clock and then quickly tiptoed into the servants' hall. Mrs Watling was still asleep, the newspaper covering her lap like a papery rug. "I'm coming," I whispered, tiptoeing back.

"Come on, then."

We bounded into the yard outside like a couple of puppies. I hadn't been outside all day and it was only then I realised how stifled and claustrophobic I'd felt. Verity and I tore across the gravel, trying to fight down our giggles. One of the groundskeepers was clipping the beech hedge that edged the kitchen garden and he whistled at us as we ran past. Verity stuck her tongue out at him.

We skidded to a halt as we came to the edge of the lawn. I could just see the black back of the inspector as he made his way into the lime tree walk that led away to the little wilderness and the lake.

"Mrs Anstells will kill you if she sees you talking to the police," I said, sobering up. "Won't she?"

"She won't be too happy," said Verity. "She'd say I should have come to her first, not go racing off the police like someone who doesn't know their place."

"Well..." I hesitated. The last thing I wanted was for Verity to be dismissed.

Verity stuck her pointy chin out even further. She had an elf's face; a wide, white forehead and high cheekbones, tapering down to her little chin. Topped with that flaming red hair, it was a face that wasn't exactly beautiful, but it had a certain vivacity. "Let's just go round the long way. We might catch him before he gets back to the house."

Gulping down my anxiety, I followed Verity. She kept behind the high hedges, out of sight of the main house. She obviously knew these grounds a lot better than I did, but then she had a lot more time to explore, either with Dorothy or without her. I began to feel nervous again, mainly about the fact that I was now supposed to be back in the kitchen. I kept following Verity, though.

We caught up with the inspector just as he was turning back along the path that led to the terrace at the back of the house.

"Sir," Verity panted, slightly out of breath from our dash. "I was hoping to speak to you, sir."

If the inspector was surprised at her forwardness, he didn't show it. In our brief interview before, he'd struck me as an astute judge of character – I suppose it went hand in hand with his job. Perhaps Verity had already impressed him during their earlier meeting. "What can I do for you, ladies?"

By now, Verity had regained her composure. "I have some information that I think would be very important for the investigation, sir."

The inspector's eyebrows rose. "Indeed? That sounds quite serious."

Verity looked sober. "Yes, I think so, sir. Given the gravity of the situation."

The inspector glanced at his watch, and in his doing so, I caught sight of the time. I really *had* to get back to the kitchen. "Well, Miss – Hunter, isn't it? Would you like to talk to me here or shall we proceed back to the house?"

Before Verity could open her mouth to answer him, I grabbed her sleeve. "V, I *must* get back. I'm so sorry." I looked at the inspector and bobbed a curtsey. "Please excuse me, sir, I'm wanted in the kitchens."

Verity gave me a pleading look but it was no use. I had to get back or risk my place. Trying to convey all of this through my facial expressions, whilst simultaneously attempting a respectful and sober face for the benefit of the inspector, would have taxed Charlie Chaplin himself. I probably just ended up looking like a lunatic. Then I bobbed another hasty curtsey and took off at a gallop for the kitchens.

"Where have you been?" Mrs Watling said sharply as I skidded into the kitchen, red in the face with exertion.

"I'm so sorry, I lost track of time." I swiped my arm across my sweating forehead, feeling resentful at her tone. The *hours* of my life that I spent in this kitchen, the hard work that I put in...it seemed as if none of that counted against five minutes' tardiness. I reached for a clean apron, trying to think of something else apologetic to say that would get past the block of resentment that currently sat in my throat.

"Well, get on with your work and we'll say no more about it," Mrs Watling said, in a slightly more mollified voice. Perhaps she was thinking what I was thinking.

"Thank you," I said, trying to sound sincere. I looked up at the menu board where Mrs Watling wrote up the meals for the day in chalk. Tonight, the family were having tomato and olive soup, followed by pork cutlets dressed with dill and cucumber, fried potatoes, honeyed carrots and parsnips, and then home-made vanilla ice-cream for pudding. As was usual, I marvelled at the decadent amount of food, the sheer excess of it all. Just one of the meals that the gentry had eaten today would have filled the bellies of five or six of the poor families in the village. Such a frivolous waste of money...but then, it was keeping me in a job, so what right did I have to complain? I took down a chopping board, collected the bowl of tomatoes, and began chopping up the fruits in a dim sort of mood.

Chapter Eight

I DIDN'T GET A CHANCE TO talk to Verity until the next morning, when we were washing and dressing in our room. She'd had to accompany Dorothy out the night before and hadn't got back until the small hours, when I was fast asleep. She was heavy-eyed that morning, yawning frequently. I helped her do her hair and make-up.

"Thank you, Joanie," she said, tipping her head back and closing her eyes as I brushed her hair.

"So, how did you get on with the inspector?"

That made her sit up and open her eyes. "Well, I told him about the gloves. I said I was absolutely certain that they weren't there first thing in the morning and that they must have been put there during the morning, while Peter was with Dorothy."

I carefully slid the pins into her hair, smoothing it under my fingers. "So did you actually say that someone else must have put them there?"

Verity made a face. "Not exactly that. I mean, it would have looked as though I was trying to tell him his job, wouldn't it?" I had to agree. "He's not stupid, Joan. He'll come to that conclusion by himself."

I slid the last pin into place. "There, done. Yes, I'm sure you're right. Listen, there's something I need to talk to you about." I glanced over at the little alarm clock that stood on our bedside table. "Lord, we're going to be late; it'll have to be later. Come on, V."

We found out something else after breakfast. Apparently the post mortem had been performed on her ladyship, and, in the usual manner of servants' gossip, the facts about it were already circulating, despite Mr Fenwick and Mrs Anstell's attempts to stop it.

"There were *splinters*," Maggie whispered to me in the pantry as we gathered the ingredients for the minestrone planned for that day's lunch. "In her *head*."

"How horrible," I said with distaste. "Don't let Mrs Watling catch you talking about it, mind."

"Yes, but Joan, think about it. Doesn't that mean someone must have hit her with one of the logs in the library fireplace?"

"I suppose so." I hurried her over to the kitchen table and started her chopping the onions. "Don't let's talk about it anymore, all right?"

Maggie crimped up her mouth, clearly longing to pick over the grisly facts a bit longer. I began seasoning the lamb, which was going to be the main course for luncheon, thinking about what Maggie had told me. Her supposition that the murder weapon had to have been one of the library logs seemed accurate. Did that mean the murder was not premeditated? Surely using a lump of wood as a weapon meant that the murderer clearly hadn't planned to do it? Didn't it?

I shook my head in impatience at myself. What business was it of mine? I turned my attention back to the food beneath my hands, trying to keep my mind on the job and off the murder.

Verity came down to lunch and we managed to sit together. The order of precedent wasn't always firmly observed at the servants' table, something for which I was thankful because it gave us a chance to talk.

"Where did you go last night?" I asked.

Verity yawned and covered her mouth. "Oh, sorry. We went to La Petite Bouche." This was a restaurant in Buxton. "I had to wait for her in the cloakroom for two bloody hours while she had a nice meal with that Simon."

"Which Simon?"

"You remember. Simon Snailer."

I remembered the name. "Oh, so she's still seeing him then? What's he like?"

Verity grinned. "Let's just say it's probably

just as well Lady E isn't here anymore. She would definitely not have approved."

I half laughed, although I was a little shocked. "In what way?"

"Well, he's got no money, for starters. He's a gentleman but he's not highborn in any way. And he looks very much like a disreputable artist."

"Is that what he is?"

"I think so. A painter, or something like that." Verity put her knife and fork neatly in the middle of her plate and took a drink of water. "That was lovely food, Joanie. Thank you."

"It was nothing," I said, but I was pleased. It was nice to have some acknowledgement of the time and effort I put into my work. I certainly wasn't going to get it from anyone upstairs, that was for sure.

Lowering my voice, I told Verity about what Maggie had mentioned to me. "Had you heard?"

Verity looked sombre. "Yes. Dorothy's been obsessing about it. Well, that's hardly surprising really, is it?"

"So, what do you think?"

"What?"

I hesitated, feeling it was a little indelicate even to be talking about it. "If the – the murder weapon was one of the logs, doesn't that indicate that it wasn't planned? I mean, it's not a very likely weapon, is it?"

Verity was chewing her lip. She rotated her

teacup on its saucer, obviously thinking. "Actually, Joanie, in some ways it's the perfect weapon. Why do you think they haven't found it yet?"

"Haven't they?" I realised I'd raised my voice in my surprise and that Mrs Anstells was starting to cast glances our way. I spoke more quietly. "How do you know that?"

"Dorothy told me. The inspector told *her*."

"Oh. Well, why haven't they found it yet?"

Verity gave me an exasperated look. "Because whoever did it probably put it straight in the fire afterwards. It's all been burnt up. Nicely concealing things like fingerprints."

I frowned. "Would you be able to get fingerprints from a piece of firewood?"

"Oh, I don't know. But my point is, that even though on the surface it doesn't look premeditated, it doesn't actually mean that it wasn't."

Mrs Anstells was definitely looking now. "No, no, you're right," I said hastily. "Let's talk about it more tonight."

After lunch, Mr Fenwick asked me to go and help the footmen clear the dining room. Slightly resentfully, because that wasn't really my job, I clambered up the stairs to the ground floor of the house and went into the dining room. Andrew and Albert were already stacking the trolley that would be rolled into the service lift for transportation to the kitchen for washing up.

There was still an awful lot of food left. No doubt, it would be mine and Mrs Watling's job to refashion the leftovers into the evening meal for the servants. Sighing inwardly, I began to clear plates from the dining table.

The doorbell rang. Both men and I looked up in surprise. The dining room stood off the entrance hall to the house and, after a moment, I could hear Mr Fenwick's ponderous footsteps wending their way to the front door. It gave that distinctive two-tone creak as he opened it.

"Good afternoon. I'm here to see Lady Dorothy." It was a man's voice, rather drawling and affected. The two footmen and I exchanged a look.

"And whom might I say is calling?" Mr Fenwick asked.

"Simon Snailer."

Alight with curiosity, I put the plate in my hand back on the table and moved closer to the door. I could feel the glances of the two men hit my back but I ignored them.

There were footsteps outside, lighter than Mr Fenwick's. Then Dorothy spoke. "Simon! You're early."

"I didn't want to keep you waiting."

As I watched, I saw them both walk past the half-open dining room door. Simon Snailer was tall and broad-shouldered, with a shaggy mop of dark hair and a moustache. He looked rather louche and

I remembered what Verity had said about him. His clothes, in the brief glimpse that I had, were shabby and paint-marked. He wore a worn tweed jacket and no tie. Mr Fenwick followed the two of them, radiating disapproval.

Their footsteps faded from hearing and I turned reluctantly back to the dining table.

"Nosy," Andrew said, grinning. I rolled my eyes at him.

Verity was in the kitchen when I got back, sitting at the table with a bottle of oil, a heap of red rose petals and some salt.

"What are you doing?" I asked, curious.

"Mixing up a potion," said Verity absently, occupied with shredding rose petals.

"It smells nice," I said, sniffing appreciatively.

Mrs Watling came bustling over and shrieked. "What knife are you using, Verity? Oh, no, no, not that one!" She pulled it out of Verity's hand. "This one's just for meat. Oh, I wished you'd asked me."

"Sorry," Verity said, annoyance edging her tone. "Which one can I use, then?"

Mrs Watling slapped a knife down in front of her. "This one. And you'll need to hurry up because we need the table for prep soon."

"All right," Verity muttered. She gathered up the rose petals and dumped them into the bowl in front of her. Then she poured over the oil and began to mix it all together with the knife.

"Is this for Dorothy?" I asked, fascinated.

Verity nodded. "This is all part of being a top-notch lady's maid. You have to be able to mix up beauty potions, do her hair, do her make-up, do her manicures and pedicures."

"Lord, I wouldn't know where to start."

Verity grinned. "Stick to cooking, Joanie. You're good at it."

"Verity—" warned Mrs Watling.

"I'm going. I'm going." Verity gathered her things together. She gave me a look and inclined her head very slightly to one side.

I followed her out of the room. "What's the matter?"

"Was there something you wanted to talk about? You said so, this morning."

For a moment, I couldn't think of what she meant, but then I remembered. I glanced around at the open kitchen door and gestured for Verity to follow me. We walked further down the corridor to where we couldn't be overheard.

"What is it?" Verity asked.

I spoke in a low tone. "Have you – have you ever seen anything strange going on between Lord Cartwright and Rosalind?"

Verity's eyes widened. "Lord Cartwright and Rosalind?" I saw her gaze go off to the side as she obviously sifted back through her memories. "By strange, do you mean—"

I nodded at her raised eyebrows. "Yes, *that*. Have you ever seen or heard anything?"

Verity looked sombre. "Why are you asking, Joanie? Have *you* seen anything?"

I told her what I'd heard – or not heard – in the study. "Of course, I could be completely mistaken. But...I don't know – it's odd."

Verity frowned. "I can't say I've ever seen anything. But—" She paused dramatically. "It wouldn't surprise me in the slightest if she *was* setting her cap at him. Now he's widowed. She'd probably love to get her feet under the table. You know how rich he is."

"Mmm." I didn't say what I was thinking, which was that Lord Cartwright would need all the money he had to make up for his unfortunate personal attributes. Not to mention his horrible temper.

"What do you—" Verity began but then we both heard Mrs Watling calling for me.

"Blast, I'll have to go."

"Me too." Verity picked up the bowl that she'd placed on the sideboard. "But I'll tell you what, Joan. I'm going to keep my eyes peeled."

"Good. Talk to you later, then."

I watched her walk up the stairs to the ground floor, trailing the scent of rose petals in her wake. Then I walked back to the kitchen, bracing myself for the hours of hard work that were yet to come.

Chapter Nine

AS WELL AS PREPARATIONS FOR dinner, I also had to prepare food and drink for afternoon tea. There was an extra person to cater for, in the form of Simon Snailer. It was Albert's afternoon off so I helped Alfred carry the tea things up to the drawing room. As I carefully carried the tray, teacups and saucers chinking together musically, I remembered doing the same all those days ago, when Lady Eveline had still been alive. I tried to feel a bit sorry at her death but she'd been such an unpleasant person, it was hard to feel much of anything. I felt sorry for Dorothy, though, and for Peter. Especially for Peter, if it were true that he was innocent.

It was a shock to see him in the drawing room. He was sitting with Dorothy and Rosalind, and they were both cooing over him as if he'd been away for years. Lord Cartwright was sat opposite them all, staring at them without expression.

"I knew they'd made a mistake," Dorothy exclaimed. "The police are just so stupid. I tried to tell them they'd made a mistake but did they listen?"

"I highly doubt the police are stupid," said Duncan. He was standing by the fire, smoking a cigarette and staring into the flames. "I get the impression that the inspector, for example, is a very sharp and calculating man."

Dorothy made a noise of disbelief. "Well, I think it's absolutely ludicrous that they arrested Peter. Anyone with half a brain could see that he had nothing to do with it."

"So who *did* do it, then?" Duncan asked with a hard tone. He threw his cigarette butt into the fire with a jerk of the wrist.

There was a shocked silence. I was pouring out the tea and the tinkle of the liquid into the cups sounded very loud. Hurriedly, I put down the pot.

"Duncan, that is not a subject for discussion in this room," said Lord Cartwright heavily.

"That's right," said Rosalind. "*Pas devant les domestiques* and all that."

It made me laugh inwardly when our betters said things like that. Did they honestly believe that we didn't understand what they were saying, just because they said it in French? I didn't know much French, although Verity was trying to teach me, but I damn well knew what that phrase meant.

I saw Duncan look at Rosalind with dislike. "Nobody asked you to stick your oar in. Why are you here, anyway? You're not part of this family, no matter how much you might like to think you are."

I saw Rosalind's face contract with shock, just before Lord Cartwright thundered "Duncan! Apologise at once."

Duncan half laughed, bitterly. Then he walked out of the room shaking his head.

I could see Rosalind trying to pretend it didn't matter. Dorothy looked uncomfortable, Peter likewise, and Simon Snailer frankly amused.

"I must apologise for my son, Rosalind, my dear," said Lord Cartwright, rather redder in the face than was normal. "He didn't mean it, I'm sure."

"It really doesn't matter," Rosalind said, with a bright, insincere smile. "We're all rather tightly wound at the moment, aren't we? It's been a very great strain."

By now I'd poured the tea out into the cups. This should really have been the time to leave the room and go back down to the kitchen but I was too curious to do that. Instead I stepped back a little from the tea table to stand against the wall next to Alfred. I dipped my head a little and clasped my hands in front of me but kept my gaze on the family.

One by one, they drifted over to pick up their tea. I got a faint smile and a 'thank you, Joan' from Dorothy, but that was it. Peter Drew looked as though he were in a not particularly pleasant dream. Rosalind was clearly still stewing over

Duncan's rude remarks. Lord Cartwright didn't bother coming up to the table. Instead he snapped his fingers at Alfred. "Get me a whisky," was all that he said.

Alfred hurried over to the drinks cabinet. I stood, demurely, watching people's faces. Simon Snailer came over and helped himself to an enormous number of scones, cakes and sandwiches. Then he went and sat back down next to Dorothy. I looked at him curiously, wondering what it was that she saw in him. He clearly didn't have money, he wasn't titled, so what was it? He was good-looking enough, in a scruffy kind of way, so perhaps that was it.

Alfred handed Lord Cartwright his whisky and came back to stand next to me by the wall. I watched Lord Cartwright. His eyes were frequently on Rosalind, although she didn't seem to notice. That fake smile had fallen off her face and she was sipping determinedly at her tea, her eyes unfocused. I wondered what she was thinking.

After ten minutes, I couldn't put off going back downstairs any longer. Nothing much was happening in the drawing room anyway. Simon sat talking to Dorothy, Peter stood by the window looking out, and Rosalind and Lord Cartwright both remained silent.

I thought Verity might have to accompany Dorothy out again that night, but luckily, that didn't turn out to be the case. I was brushing my hair out in front of our little mirror when she came into the bedroom.

"I thought you'd be out tonight," I said, catching her eye in the mirror.

"So did I, but Dorothy changed her mind." Verity sat down on her bed with a thankful sigh and unbuckled her shoes. "Ooh, my feet. I feel like I've been on them all day."

"Is Simon Snailer staying the night?" I asked.

Verity giggled. "Yes, he is. Wonder if there'll be some late night corridor wandering later?"

"Verity!" I had to admit, I was a little shocked. "Would Dorothy do that?"

"I wouldn't put it past her," she said, still smiling. "She's a modern woman, remember?"

"She'd better hope Lord C doesn't find out," I remarked, laying the brush back down on the tiny dressing table. "He'd throw her out of the house."

"Well, maybe he's got a few secrets of his own," said Verity. She lay back on her pillow, smiling cynically. "I think you might be right about him and Rosalind."

"Do you?" I turned in my seat. "I was watching him today in the drawing room at tea. He did look at her a lot."

Verity yawned and sat back up. "Lord, I am so tired. I must get to bed." She heaved herself to her feet and started to undress. "God knows what Dorothy is going to want to do tomorrow."

What we'd been talking about went out of my head, given my concentration on getting my hair pinned up properly. Verity took her washbag and went down the hall to the servants' bathroom to brush her teeth. When she came back, I was already tucked into my bed with the covers pulled cosily up to my chin.

It was only when she turned down the lamp that it occurred to me. "V..." I said, slowly.

"What is it?" came her drowsy voice through the darkness.

"If – and I know we don't know for certain – *if* Lord Cartwright is involved with Rosalind—" I broke off, uncertain of whether I actually dared put my thoughts into words.

"What?" Verity's sleepy voice said.

I took a deep breath. "Well, then that gives him a motive, doesn't it?"

There was a moment of silence. Then Verity, sounding more awake, said "My God, Joan. You're right. It does."

We were both quiet. Then I said, uncertainly, "It can't be, though, can it? I mean, surely he's the first person the police would suspect. Remember Asharton?"

"How could I forget?" Verity sounded completely awake now. I heard a rustle as she sat up in bed and then the rattle of the matchbox. As she re-lit the lamp, there was a flare of light against the darkness that made me screw up my eyes.

Verity was looking at me intently, so intently she almost scared me. "What is it?" I said, nervously.

"I was talking about this with Dorothy," Verity said slowly. "A few days after it happened, when she'd calmed down a bit. She'd had to tell the police where she was between eleven thirty at night and five and twenty past one in the morning."

Her stare was still unsettling me. "So what did she tell them?"

"Dorothy said she'd got in from Dickie Fotherington-Gill's party at about one o'clock. She said she was a bit vague about the time because she'd had a few too many cocktails."

I half laughed. "Well, she had, hadn't she? I remember you telling me."

"That was something I had to confirm to the police – they asked me whether she was telling the truth."

There was something quite shocking in that – the idea that a lady's maid would be asked to essentially betray her mistress, if in fact, her lady had been telling an untruth. I began to feel nervous again. "So, was Dorothy being truthful?"

"Yes, of course she was. I helped her into bed at about ten past one. So unless she got up again immediately after I'd left her and went down to the library..." Verity trailed off, chewing her lip.

I understood her hesitation. It was a horrible thought, a daughter doing that brutality to her mother. I just couldn't see Dorothy doing such a hideous thing. Would she even have had the strength to wield a heavy piece of wood in that fashion?

"Anyway," Verity continued after a moment. "I've strayed off the point a little. The fact is that Dorothy told me that both her step-father and Rosalind had an alibi, because they'd been working late together in the study that evening."

I laughed cynically. "Working, they say?"

Verity smiled weakly. "Well, that's what they said. But you know, Joanie, Rosalind must be telling the truth – about being in the study, anyway – because I saw her."

I stared at her. "Really?"

Verity nodded vigorously. "Dorothy had spilt one of those really sticky cocktails all down her dress, and I wanted to get it in to soak before the stain set. I was coming down the back corridor, you know, that runs past the study and there was a light on in the room. I looked – well, you do, don't you? And Rosalind was sitting at the desk, writing something down."

"What time was this?" I asked.

"It must have been at least twenty past one. There just wouldn't have been time for her to...to do it. Not to mention that she's tiny. Lady E towered over her. Would Rosalind have had the strength to do it?"

That echoed precisely those thoughts I'd just had about Dorothy. Verity and I looked at each other for a moment. Then Verity added, "I told the police that too."

"So they must know that she's speaking the truth," I said quietly.

Verity nodded. "So does that mean they think Lord Cartwright is in the clear as well?"

Suddenly exhausted, I leant my head back against the flaking plaster of the wall behind me, despite knowing I'd end up with flakes in my hair. "I don't know, V. I don't know."

There was a short pause and then Verity said, "Look, it's too late to discuss this now. Let's see what we can find out tomorrow and see if that takes us any further."

"Agreed," I said. I could feel my eyelids drooping. We both slid down under our respective covers again.

"Good night, Joanie," came her tired voice from across the room as she reached out to the lamp.

"Good night."

Chapter Ten

I WOKE UP THE NEXT MORNING with a feeling of gladness, and for a moment I couldn't think why. Then I remembered. Today was Sunday, and this afternoon was my afternoon off. Even better, I knew Verity had arranged to have her afternoon off at the same time. After lunch, and after I'd prepared the afternoon tea, we'd be able to leave Merisham Lodge, walk into Merisham, and go for tea somewhere.

I almost bounced out of bed and hurried to wash myself and get dressed. The water in the servants' washroom was never more than lukewarm but I didn't let it bother me. When I got back to our room, Verity was just waking up. She had the luxury of a much later start time than I did, although, to be fair, sometimes she had to wait up or work into the early hours, unlike me, so I suppose it evened out in the end.

Quickly I started pinning up my hair, realising I had only one clean cap left. I would have to do some washing later. Verity groaned, yawned and slowly extracted herself from the bedclothes.

"Have you thought about where you want to go this afternoon?" I asked, catching her eye in the mirror.

"What?" she said sleepily. Then comprehension dawned. "Oh, yes, it's our afternoon off. Oh, hurray for that! Let's go to the good tea-shop, Joanie, why not? Let's treat ourselves to a nice cake and someone else serving us for once."

"That sounds wonderful." I rammed the last pin home, straightened the frill over my forehead, and got up.

I was at the bedroom door when Verity spoke again. "Joan. Do you remember what we talked about last night?"

I hadn't but then, of course, it all came back to me. "Yes, of course I do."

Verity picked up her shawl and washbag. "Well, I'm going to do my best this morning to find out who had what alibi. Then we can discuss it later over tea."

"Good idea." For a moment, I felt a strange reluctance to do so. Was it really our place, after all? We weren't policemen. We weren't even members of the family. So why *were* we so interested?

I said goodbye and began the long journey down four flights of the servants' stairs. Why *were* we so interested? I had overhead Rosalind and

Peter Drew talking a few days ago, on the stairs as I passed by in the corridor below. Rosalind had said something like, "*Of course, the servants' hall is positively buzzing with gossip. People of that class can be complete ghouls, can't they?*" And Peter had replied, "*Well, it's probably because they don't have anything else to occupy their minds with, what?*"

They'd heard my footsteps then and stopped talking abruptly as I walked past beneath them. I remembered how my face had burnt as hot as fire, but I'd said nothing; of course I'd said nothing. I'd just kept walking down to the safe confines of the kitchen. It was Peter's comment that made me particularly angry. Didn't have anything to occupy our minds with? Apart from making sure he and his family lived in unimaginable comfort, ease and luxury, that is?

I stomped into the kitchen in a bad mood, forgetting entirely that it was only six hours before I'd have an afternoon of relative freedom. I busied myself with getting the range good and hot, putting the kettle on for Mrs Watling's cup of tea, and beginning the preparations for breakfast.

Mrs Watling came in shortly after that and I had to snap out of my mood or risk her displeasure. There was something to be said for work, I suppose; it kept you occupied and stopped you sinking into too much introspection or melancholy. As I fried bacon, and the big flat mushrooms that came from a farm nearby, I thought about an interesting conversation I'd had one night, years ago now. I'd been to visit Verity when she was working at the Cartwrights' family home in London, the townhouse in Hampstead. It had been around Christmas time, and we'd all had a glass of ale in the servants' hall, which was quite a comfortable one with a good fire. Perhaps that's why all the servants were a bit more chatty than normal. Even Mr Fenwick had unbent a little. Everyone started talking about the more eccentric families that they'd worked for, or the strange individuals they had served. Soon, it became almost a game, with maids and footmen coming out with more and more outrageous stories. I, being a visitor at the time, hadn't put myself forward but I'd listened with great interest. I was new in service then and hadn't seen much, but here were tales of the master who, regular as clockwork, would get drunk, come downstairs to the kitchen and start hurling both insults and plates at the kitchen maids. "'Filthy harlots, dirty strumpets!' he'd say," said Doris, one of the kitchen maids, almost choking with laughter. "And then Cook, bless her soul, would turn around and give him such a tongue-lashing back until he ran out with his tail between his legs. Oh, she was a caution!"

Of course, I'd sat there with eyes like saucers, scarcely able to believe such stories. When Mr Fenwick retired to his own room, the anecdotes got a little bit saucier. One of the footmen told us a scandalous tale about the chauffeur to one of the most famous families amongst the gentry, who was managing to have an affair with both the master and the mistress of the house. "No!" we all cried. "That can't be true!" But the footman, Tom, assured us it was.

Of course, I was as green as grass then and didn't *really* know what he was talking about. I remembered discussing it all with Verity that night as we said goodbye at the kitchen door before I left to go back to where I was in service myself.

"There seems to be an awful lot of strange, high-born folk around," I'd said. "What makes them all so eccentric?"

Verity had given me a strange look, half disbelieving, half sympathetic. "I would have thought it was obvious, Joanie."

"In what way do you mean?"

Verity chuckled. "Look, I know we hate work, but it gives us a purpose, doesn't it? It means we get up and we've actually got something to do. Can you imagine what it's actually like to do *nothing*, all day? All year? For the whole of your life? People aren't designed to do nothing all day, are they? It does something to your mind, I think, to know that you're absolutely useless, that you can't even take care of yourself. No, it's much better to have work than not have it. Really."

I had stared at her, amazed. The thought that perhaps we, the servants, were in fact fortunate in this way had never, ever occurred to me.

I thought about that often, after our conversation. Although I couldn't quite give up my envy of those who had so much, when I had so little, the memory of Verity's explanation came in as a comfort sometimes, when the hard work seemed endless and the days so long. Not much of a comfort, but a little.

Remembering this, I brightened somewhat. An extra cup of tea after breakfast helped and then Mrs Watling and I set to with a will to produce the Sunday roast. The family nearly always went to church on Sunday mornings and it gave the house a decently empty feel.

After lunch had been served, cleared away and washed up, I set to, preparing the tray for tea. Once the sandwiches had been cut and the scones had been buttered, I covered them with a damp tea towel, put the little lids on the glass pots that contained the honey, marmalade and fish paste and gave a last polish to the empty silver teapot that stood awaiting its filling, nearer the time. Maggie would see to it in my absence. Then, feeling happiness fill me up again, I took the stairs upstairs as fast as I could, to get quickly washed and changed out of my uniform.

Verity wasn't there but she was waiting at the kitchen door for me when I got back downstairs.

She had on a green velvet cloche hat that Dorothy had given her, which made the red-gold of her hair stand out most attractively. I could see my own happiness and excitement reflected in her face.

We didn't speak until we were out of the lodge grounds and climbing over the stile to the footpath that wound through the fields.

"Oh my Lord, Joanie, it's good to be out of there." Verity threw her head back, squeezing her eyes closed for a second.

"I know what you mean." It was difficult to walk soberly, as we were expected to do. I felt like running and jumping and spinning around, so glad was I to be free.

"When do you have to be back?"

"Not until seven o'clock."

"Wonderful." Verity slipped her hand about my arm and gave it a squeeze. "Because I have lots to tell you."

As we walked towards Merisham, I found myself thinking of Asharton Manor. It had never been very far from my thoughts over the past week, ever since the murder had happened. That was strange, because after the murder at Asharton Manor, and for a while after I'd left the place, it was as if it had all been a strange and terrifying dream. I had to remind myself that it had actually happened. I think it was when the case came to court that it became real to me again. Perhaps it was the flaring black headlines in the papers every day. *Evil Killers. Depravity at Asharton Manor. Murderers Hanged.* It made it difficult to forget or to dismiss it as a dream.

"Penny for them, Joan?"

I started. Without me realising, we had reached the high street of Merisham and Verity was steering me in the direction of one of the three tea shops available. This one, Peggy's Parlour, was the most expensive but had the most delicious cakes.

We went inside and were shown to a table at the back. I didn't mind. We were near the entrance to the kitchens. It was rather noisier than it would have been at the window tables, but that would make it easier to talk without being overhead. It made me feel a little uneasy, the fact that I was thinking like that. It was like Asharton Manor, all over again. But along with the uneasiness was another feeling, the same one I'd felt back then. Excitement. A sense of purpose. The fact that Verity and I were facing a challenge, again.

Verity ordered such a variety of cakes that I was quite alarmed.

"Verity, are you sure..."

She waved away my concerns. "Of course. Don't worry. Dorothy gave me a couple of extra shillings the other night."

"Why?"

Verity's mouth quirked up at the corners. "I

think it was because I made sure she got back to her room in time for breakfast."

I felt my eyes widened. "Back to her room?"

Verity giggled. "Well, yes. Because that Simon stayed the night, didn't he?"

I could feel myself blushing, absurdly. It was ridiculous, it wasn't as if I were some giggly teenager anymore, and what was Dorothy's love life to me? I think I was just awe-struck at her nerve.

I leant forward. "Isn't she afraid of – well, you know. Getting into trouble?"

Verity shook her head. "There are ways and means, Joanie," she said, mysteriously to me. "Anyway. That's enough about her, for now."

The tea and cakes came then, and the next few minutes were occupied with pouring our tea, pressing cakes upon each other and then taking the first satisfying sip.

After the first cake, Verity daintily wiped her mouth and leant forward a little.

"So," she said, with a little more urgency in her voice. "I got talking to Dorothy about the police. She's furious with them because of them arresting Peter."

"They *did* release him," I protested.

Verity waved a hand impatiently. "I know that. It's just that it makes it quite easy to get Dorothy going on the subject. She gets very indignant."

I helped myself to another cake. The waitress

came up and topped up our teapot with hot water and I gave her a grateful smile. It felt so good to be waited on for a change.

"Well," I said as soon as my mouth was clear of cake crumbs. "He is her brother, after all, despite the fact she obviously thinks he's a complete no-hoper."

Verity was pouring tea as I said that and she suddenly frowned. "It's funny you say that," she said, putting down the tea pot.

"Why is that?"

"Something that Dorothy told me. She'd been talking to Peter about what he was going to do for money now – you know how he's always got none. It was funny but she said something like 'he told me he's got some money coming to him soon so he'll be all right.'"

I waited but Verity didn't say any more. "And?" I prompted.

"Well, that's just it. Dorothy seemed – seemed a bit nonplussed. A bit puzzled. As if she couldn't imagine where Peter would be getting this mysterious money."

It seemed obvious to me. "What about the will?" I asked quietly.

Verity looked at me startled. "The will?"

It wasn't like Verity to be so slow. "The will," I repeated. "Her ladyship's will."

Verity's frown cleared. "Oh, *that*. Joanie, you genius, of course it must be that. How could I not have guessed?" She picked up the teapot again and topped up my cup. "I'll tell Dorothy that tonight, take her mind off it."

"I suppose the will has already been read?" I asked.

Verity shrugged. "I don't think it has, actually. I'm sure I overheard Rosalind making an appointment with the solicitors. I think they're coming during the week."

We were down to our last cake by now and of course, we each urged the other to have it. "Let's split it," Verity said, brandishing a knife.

We each took a piece and munched away. I drained the dregs of my tea cup, wondering if I was going to tell Verity what was on my mind.

"I've been thinking a lot about Asharton Manor," I said after a moment. Verity looked up from her plate, quickly. "I suppose it's inevitable, given the circumstances."

"Yes," she said, slowly.

Now it was my turn to look down. "We did – we did do the right thing, didn't we, V?"

Verity looked astonished. "How can you even ask that? Of course we did!"

"I know," I said, uncertainly. Not for the first time I wished I had Verity's strength of character, her firm and sound knowledge of her own mind. She didn't sway this way and that, like me. She wasn't *wishy-washy*.

At Asharton Manor, the evidence Verity and I had found had led to the hanging of two people. It was a thought that sometimes woke me up at night – that I, Joan Hart, lowly kitchen maid, could be said to be responsible for the deaths of two people.

Of course, Verity, when I'd once confessed I sometimes felt like that, had given me a stern talking to. Of course it wasn't down to us. If people didn't want to be hanged for murder, then perhaps they shouldn't commit murders. I knew she was right, but...

That was what was making me drag my feet a little now. Fleetingly, I wondered whether in both cases if the murder victim had been – well, a bit nicer – I'd feel differently about catching their killer.

I thrust the thought of that horrid old manor house from my mind and turned my attention back to what Verity was saying.

"So I had it from Benton that Duncan was listening to the wireless in the snug until after half past one that night. Probably getting stuck into the whisky as well, knowing him."

I forced myself to take an interest. "So, that clears him really, doesn't it? How did you get Benton to tell you?" Benton was Duncan Cartwright's valet and not given much to chatting with us kitchen maids. He was a good looking man of about thirty, but the sneer that always hovered around his countenance when he addressed us put me off him a bit.

Verity looked mischievous. "I used my feminine wiles."

I giggled. "Meaning?"

Verity laughed. "Actually, I hardly had to do anything. He's a bit of a goat, that one. You want to watch yourself, if you find yourself in a dark corridor with him."

"I'll bear that in mind," I said, drily. "How did Benton know he was there all evening?"

"Oh, he kept asking for things – drinks and for his cigarette box to be filled."

I sat back in my seat and used my fingers to tick people off. "So Duncan's in the clear, Dorothy's in the clear, but Rosalind and Lord Cartwright are providing each other's alibi. Is that correct?"

"Correct."

We sat and looked at each other across the table. "What about Peter? Why *did* they release him?"

Verity shrugged. "Presumably because I told them that he was with Dorothy all that time before the gloves were found in his room."

"Hmm." It was the first time I'd really considered those bloody gloves. It gave me a nasty feeling. The intent, surely, had been to cast suspicion on Peter Drew, but why? Was he just a convenient scapegoat?

It was Verity who looked up at the clock on the wall above my head and exclaimed. "Goodness, Joan,

I'm going to have to go. Dorothy's dining out with Simon again tonight and I need to get her ready."

We got up, having left the money for the tea and cakes in a convenient saucer on the table. I left an extra bit of money for the waitress. I knew what it was like to have to toil on your feet all day with no thanks.

We quickly hurried up the street and turned off to follow the footpath that led back through the fields. The sky darkened as we walked, and as we reached the stile, the first fat drops of rain began to fall, darkening the shoulders of our coats and our hats. In the end, we had to run for the kitchen door, breathlessly arriving in the kitchen in a whirl of muddy shoes and wet clothes, and there wasn't time to say anything more than a hurried goodbye before we both had to get back to work.

Chapter Eleven

Just as Verity had said, the solicitor for Lady Eveline arrived for the reading of the will on the Wednesday of the next week. Mrs Watling and I had orders to prepare a more ambitious luncheon than normal. Rosalind Makepeace had taken to coming down to discuss the menus and the orders with Mrs Watling every morning, just as Lady Eveline had done. I presumed she was doing so on Lord Cartwright's orders, but it still seemed a little bit of a liberty to me. I wasn't alone in this. After she left that Wednesday morning, Mrs Watling had sniffed and tossed her head. "Thinks she's lady of the manor already, that one does," was her only comment.

I nodded but said nothing, concentrating on making the rabbit *quenelles*. I was trying to remember Lady Eveline's attitude towards her husband's secretary. Had she been friendly with her? Or antagonistic? For the life of me, I couldn't remember.

According to Verity, the solicitor, whose name was Mr Fossick, was due to arrive at midday. When the front doorbell rang, faintly through the floorboards, at about five minutes before the hour, of course I thought it was him. But after a moment, several sets of heavy footsteps sounded up above. I looked up in consternation.

After a moment, Verity came down with Dorothy's breakfast tray, heaped with soiled dishes. "The police are here again," she whispered as she brushed past me on the way to the scullery.

Startled, I was distracted from my work for a moment. The police here? For the reading of the will? Why? As I bent to push the rabbit meat through a horsehair sieve to make it as fine as it could be, I wondered. Could it be that they wanted to watch people's faces as the will was read? Were they looking for shock, or anger, or triumph?

I wanted to be able to be there myself, to see for myself, but I knew that would be impossible. I plucked Verity's sleeve as she walked back past me. "Is there any way you can be in on the will reading?" I murmured.

Her expressive face showed what she thought of that suggestion. "Not likely. Not unless Dorothy has a fit of the vapours, or something." I saw her expression change. "Actually, that gives me an idea. Yes, that might work… Leave it with me, Joanie."

I had to be content with that. There was soup

to be clarified, roasting potatoes to turn, cheese to remove from the refrigerator. I patted the big metal box affectionately as I took out the paper-wrapped package. I'd worked in enough kitchens to really appreciate the new-fangled appliances that were slowly being introduced to the houses that could afford them. Of course, we still got daily deliveries of meat, milk, fish and vegetables, but now we could actually keep them fresh for longer than a day. It was marvellous. Right after I'd left the orphanage, I'd worked in one awful kitchen where the cook was a right, mean old skinflint. With my own eyes, I'd seen her 'wash out' a smelly, slimy chicken by sticking its backside over the gas jet and letting it fill with gas like stuffing. Then she'd lit the gas to get rid of the stench of rotting meat. *Awful.* I lost a lot of weight in that job, I can tell you. I didn't dare eat anything she'd cooked. Luckily, me and the housemaids used to steal food, when we could, and hide it in a special cupboard only we knew about.

Thinking of that horrible position made me feel rather grateful to be here now, with a reasonably sympathetic woman to work under, a decent kitchen and modern appliances to work with. I went back to the *quenelles* with a lighter heart, forgetting about the drama that was unfolding upstairs.

After the lunch was sent upstairs, and the servants' lunch was finished, both Mrs Watling and

I fortified ourselves with a cup of tea and a bun. I decided this was as good a time as any to get a bit more information on the family.

I began conventionally enough. "It's a terrible tragedy about her ladyship, isn't it, Mrs Watling?"

Mrs Watling sighed and rested her head against the high back of the chair. "I never thought I'd have to go through anything quite so shocking in my life, Joan, and that's a fact. I thought I'd go to my grave without having witnessed anything quite so awful. It makes me feel quite weak."

I knew what she meant. I was pretty sure that she wasn't mourning Lady Eveline herself – who amongst the servants could? It was the shocking nature of her death that was so difficult to comprehend – that was what was so difficult to get past. I hesitated over my next question; it was one that could be taken the wrong way. "So what – what do you think happened, Mrs Watling? Who could have done such a terrible thing?"

Mrs Watling sat up a little. "Not one of the family, if that's what you're thinking, Joan," she said sharply. "I'm sure none of them would do such an awful thing. The very thought doesn't bear thinking of." She was silent for a moment and then said reflectively, "No, it must have been an outsider. A tramp or a maniac. Some terrible person like that. There's been an awful lot of desperate men out there since the war."

I knew what she meant, but I forbad to point out that the war had ended twelve years ago. "You've worked for the family for a long time, haven't you?"

Mrs Watling sighed. "Almost twenty years, Joan. That's why I can't think—" She pushed up the rim of her cap and sighed. "I knew Master Duncan as a tiny boy. He was such a lovely child. Such golden curls and such a winning way about him. He used to come down to the kitchen for raisins and ask for them so sweetly. Of course, his mother put a stop to that once she found out, and quite rightly."

I waited. She was obviously in a reminiscing mood.

"Lord Cartwright wasn't so wealthy then but they still had to have the best of everything. My goodness, what armies of staff we had then, Joan. You would scarcely believe it. Of course, anyone who was anyone wouldn't have dreamt of having less than three footmen. I was a kitchen maid then, and the cook was a Frenchwoman, Madame Bouchard. French cooks were the fashion, then." Mrs Watling sighed again and then painfully eased herself from her chair. "What a long time ago now it seems. Another lifetime."

With a sudden painful twist, I saw what she meant. For a second, my imagination showed me a young and pretty Mrs Watling, slim in her maid's uniform, dashing hither and thither under the orders of the French cook. I looked at her now, rather stouter and greyer, and worn out from the hard work. Yes, she was a cheerful sort of woman but I realised now I knew nothing about what she'd wanted to become, what her dreams and hopes and aspirations had been. I saw myself, twenty years from now, doing the same thing. I would be 'Mrs Hart' but I would not be married. I would not have any children. I would have spent my entire youth slaving over a baking hot stove, making sure the fat, lazy people up above wanted for nothing, while down below my life went up in smoke and down the drain.

Shaken, I forgot about asking more about the family. Silently the two of us got up and moved towards the kitchen table, our hands reaching automatically for the pots on the stove, the utensils on the chopping board. My throat closed up. All of a sudden, the kitchen felt stifling, its walls closing about me.

"Just got to get a bit of air," I mumbled and staggered towards the door to the courtyard outside. I saw Mrs Watling look at me in surprise but by then, I had reached the steps and run up them, to stand out in the courtyard, tipping my face up to the sky and taking deep breaths of clean, cold air.

Of course, I had to go back down eventually. By that time, though, I'd calmed down. I walked back downstairs, determined to do what I'd originally set out to do today. All my earlier qualms about whether it was my place to start investigating had disappeared. All right, if I was going to be a kitchen maid for the rest of my life, I'd damn well start keeping my mind occupied with other things. Otherwise I'd end up like Mrs Watling, chained to the kitchen sink and, even worse, not even realising I'd ended up in prison.

I put on a clean apron and began briskly preparing the potatoes for the evening meal. These had to be chopped very finely, so that when you held up a slice to the light, you could almost see through it. These slices would be cooked very quickly in boiling hot fat and come out (if you got them out in time) beautifully crisp and golden, and to be eaten in one satisfyingly crunchy bite.

After a few minutes, I said pleasantly, "I'm so sorry, Mrs Watling, you were telling me about working for the family for so long. It was very interesting. What was Lord Cartwright's first wife like?"

If that was a bit of a non-sequitur, Mrs Watling didn't seem to notice. She was spiking the pork joint all over with rosemary twigs and basting it with pork fat. "Lady Alice? Oh, she was a lovely lady. Quite different to Lady Eveline, God rest her. She – Lady Alice, I mean – she was very beautiful and very soft in her manner. Not strong though, physically. Nobody expected her to make old bones."

Mrs Watling jabbed the last sprig of rosemary into the meat and sighed. "And she didn't, poor soul."

"It was an accident, wasn't it?" I asked.

"She fell down the stairs, the poor woman." Mrs Watling shook her head.

"Here?" I said.

"No, no, in the townhouse." She meant the Hampstead house. "A stair rod had come loose, or there was a bit of loose carpet – something like that – and she caught her foot in it one night and fell down. That was a terrible night, and no mistake." Mrs Watling went to put the pork joint in the refrigerator. The door squeaked, as if underlining her words. "It took me right back, I can tell you, seeing the police here after Lady Eveline was...after she died. Of course, Lady Alice's death was nothing but a tragic accident but, well, it gave me a nasty turn, having to remember it."

She bustled off into the pantry and left me with my pile of translucent potato slices. I transferred them all to a pot of cold, salted water and rinsed the chopping board in the sink. So the police had been called when Lady Alice's death was discovered? Was that usual? I found I had no idea and resolved to ask Verity about it later.

During the afternoon, Dorothy rang for tea to be brought up. It would normally be one of the parlourmaids' jobs to take up the tray, but I volunteered to do it and Nora, the parlourmaid whose job it should have been, was grateful. "Thank you Joan, I owe you," she said as I picked up the tray. I winked at her and began the trip upstairs. I felt pleased with myself. I'd be able to have a quick word with Verity, perhaps even ascertain what had happened with the will reading, and I'd made a friend in Nora at the same time. As it was, I liked Nora. She was a very pretty girl, dark-haired and blue-eyed, and she had a wicked sense of humour. Once she, Verity and I had been to the talkies together and gone for tea afterwards, and she'd had us all in stitches with her droll impressions of Greta Garbo and Joan Crawford.

I knocked on the door to Dorothy's room, and Verity herself opened it. She looked surprised but pleased to see me.

I hadn't seen Dorothy since that awkward family gathering in the drawing room, when Duncan had been so rude to Rosalind. I thought Dorothy looked a little better, not quite so drawn and red-eyed as she had been for the past week. As usual, she was smoking a cigarette, this time in a long, delicately carved holder which looked as though it were made out of ivory. I placed the tea tray on the usual table by the window and Dorothy greeted me pleasantly by name. That was true breeding, I thought, and people like Rosalind would never attain it.

Verity indicated that I should pour the tea and I did so. Verity took Dorothy her cup.

"Thank you, Verity." Dorothy took a sip. "Ah, you make a wonderful cup of tea, Joan. I wouldn't even know how to boil a kettle; it's quite shocking. You'll have to show me how, one day."

I wasn't sure if she was being serious. Dorothy had that kind of deep, drawling voice that always sounds sarcastic. I'd noticed a lot of ladies affected that sort of voice, I suppose it was fashionable. "Of course, my lady," I said in a tone I hoped was wry without being cheeky.

Dorothy drained the cup, put it and the saucer back on the bedside table, and flung herself back against the headboard, putting the cigarette to her lips. "I suppose there's been ever such a kerfuffle in the servants' hall this past week? What with the police here and everything?"

It's funny but as curious as the servants can be about the gentry, you forget it sometimes worked the other way around. Particularly for people like Dorothy, who are easily bored. I remembered Verity telling me how, at her interview for the position, Dorothy had told her that one of the most important parts of the job would be to talk with the other ladies' maids and servants to see what all the gossip was. *Nobody knows the scandal better than a good servant*, Dorothy had said to Verity.

"It has been rather fraught, my lady," I said, refilling her cup.

"Ha! I can imagine. Poor Mr Fenwick must be having kittens." Dorothy reached for her replenished teacup. "Thank you, Joan. Tell me, what does Mrs Watling think about it all? I've noticed the dinners haven't been quite so up to scratch these last few days. Is she upset?"

"I'm sorry to hear that, my lady," I gabbled. "I'll be sure to tell her."

"Oh, now, don't. It's perfectly understandable under the circumstances. She must be upset. Is she, Joan?"

I nodded. "She's very shocked. Well, we all are, my lady." I hesitated, wondering whether to bring this up. "Mrs Watling said it brought back a few bad memories. You know, of when Lord Cartwright's first wife was killed."

"Killed? Oh, but that was an accident. She fell down the stairs." Dorothy ground her cigarette out in a brimming ashtray. "It wasn't a great surprise to anyone, to be honest. She drank, you know."

Coming from Dorothy, with her enormous consumption of brandy and champagne cocktails, that was a bit rich, but of course I didn't say anything about that. "Oh yes, I know that, my lady. I think it was just the shock of it, of sudden death, that reminded her." I then remembered, rather belatedly, that I was talking to a girl who'd lost her mother to murder. "I'm so sorry to talk about it though, my lady, it's not my place."

"Nonsense." But Dorothy's eyes had filled. Blinking, she looked away and lit another cigarette.

I took that as my cue to leave and began to lift the empty cups onto the tea tray. But Verity gave me the minutest shake of the head and I hesitated. She telegraphed something to me with her eyebrows, and when I hesitated some more, unsure of what she was trying to say, mouthed 'will' at me.

I took a deep breath. "Was the luncheon we prepared today to your satisfaction, my lady?"

Dorothy was smoking and staring into space. She looked up at my voice. "What's that, Joan?"

"The luncheon today – for when Mr Fossick dined with you. I hope it was satisfactory? I just wanted to know, after what you've said about the dinners, my lady, I mean."

Dorothy's frown cleared. "Oh, that. Oh yes, it was fine. To be honest, Joan, nobody really felt like eating much. We were all too nervous about the will."

She stopped speaking but in that way that you get the impression they want to go on, just with a bit of prompting. So I said, "The will, my lady?"

"My mother's will. That's why Mr Fossick was here today, to read her will." Dorothy spoke to me as if this would have never occurred to me and I tried not to mind. "Golly, out of all the horrible things that have happened over the past couple of weeks, at least that *was* a relief."

"Was it, my lady?" I couldn't quite believe she was being so forthcoming but then Dorothy never had been that discreet.

"Oh yes. Didn't I say? I thought Mother might have cut me out of her will. She always threatened to, if I persisted in seeing Simon. I actually thought she'd really *done* it, this time. But then, she hadn't. Or perhaps she hadn't got around to it before – before she died." She stubbed out her cigarette with a jab. "Poor Mother."

I didn't quite know what to say, but I don't think she was listening to me anymore. I murmured something about 'being very glad for you in this sad time, my lady', and then I thought I'd really better leave, Verity or no Verity.

I closed the door softly behind me and began to make my way back to the servants' stairs. The corridor curved sharply at a right angle, leading around to where Duncan's and Lord Cartwright's bedrooms were located. As I walked towards the turn, I heard the sound of a door opening around the corner, and there was something about it that made my footsteps slow. As I came up to the corner, I stopped still and peered around the wall, cautiously.

A man was coming out of Duncan's bedroom. For a moment, I thought it was Benton but there was something furtive in the way he was moving that made me reassess after a moment. It was Peter Drew, I realised. What was he doing in Duncan's bedroom? He hurried away down the corridor away from me, and there was something in the set of his shoulders that recalled to me a butler I'd once known who'd spent his time at the house spying and sneaking on the people he was supposed to serve. That butler had been dismissed in the end, I remembered, because he'd poked his nose in one too many times for comfort. And here was Peter Drew, moving in exactly the same shifty, furtive way. *He's snooping*, I thought. I watched him scurry down the corridor and followed him slowly, letting him move out of sight before I turned the corner.

Chapter Twelve

I woke up at half past five in the morning the next day, as usual. It was worse now, in the gathering gloom of autumn, when it was beginning to get so dark and cold it felt as if it were still the middle of the night. I put my feet into the slippers that Verity had given me last Christmas and wrapped my shawl around my shoulders. Then I hurried down the corridor to the servants' bathroom.

To my surprise, it was already occupied. I was used to being the first one up on this floor – Maggie was a bit of a slug-a-bed, and it was usually my second task of the day to get her up. Perhaps she'd managed the impossible and got herself up for once. I waited outside the bathroom, my need for the lavatory growing increasingly urgent. I was almost at the point of dashing back to my room to use the po' when at last the door opened. I was surprised to see Nora.

She looked a little pale, and the smile she gave me was wan. She didn't say anything though, just walked past me and back down the corridor to her room. I hurried into the vacated bathroom. The little window was wide open, letting in blasts of chilly air, and I quickly shut it, shivering.

The morning followed its usual routine – preparing the breakfasts, the clearing and washing of the pots and utensils and a quick cup of tea before the onslaught of luncheon began. Today they were having minestrone soup to begin, followed by mackerel fillets with lemon and thyme, mashed carrot, potato and swede and a dessert of peaches in chartreuse jelly and ice-cream. Followed of course by the usual fruits, coffee and cheeses.

I checked the vegetable rack – we were low on both carrots and swedes. I took a basket down from where it hung on the hooks by the back door and made my way to the root cellar. This was the darkest and dankest of the cellars, situated behind the wine cellar, right at the back of the labyrinth of corridors that lay beneath the kitchen itself. I always hated a trip down there. The only light came from a dusty bulb that hung over the stairs so the far reaches of the room were always in flickering shadow.

Quickly, I walked towards the sandboxes where the root vegetables were kept and grabbed handfuls of what I needed. I wanted to get out of this dark, spooky place as quickly as possible. It smelled horrible down here too, mouldy and dusty at the same time. I picked up the laden basket and ran up the stairs as quickly as I could, as if something nasty were snapping at my heels.

Mrs Watling darted between the gas stove-top and the range, checking on pots and prodding pans. She glanced at me as I came back into the kitchen with my vegetables and gave me a look of approval.

I was sitting at the kitchen table, scraping industriously away with my peeler when Verity came into the room with an armful of clothes and some jewellery boxes. She greeted me, Maggie and Mrs Watling and sat herself down next to me.

"Mending?" I asked.

"What else? And some jewellery to clean, too."

She opened up the nearest flat leather box. Inside was a beautiful string of pearls. I stared, fascinated, as Verity went and fetched a little glass of milk and began to clean the pearls with the milk and a soft cloth.

"Do you clean all Dorothy's jewellery?" I spoke softly so Mrs Watling wouldn't take me to task for not calling Dorothy 'her ladyship'.

"Not the really expensive stuff. That goes to a specialist. But, yes, the paste jewels, these pearls for example – they're not so valuable so she doesn't mind if I do it."

Both Mrs Watling and Maggie were otherwise occupied. I leaned in closer and murmured "So what happened with the will reading? Did you manage to get in on it?"

Verity grinned. "I persuaded Dorothy to let me come in case she had a shock and she needed me." She paused to wipe the last pearl clean and then laid the string down gently. "You know, I think she actually thought she would have one. A shock, I mean. About the will."

I thought back to what Dorothy had said. "You mean, that her mother might have cut her out because of that Simon?"

"Yes. I think she was really worried about it. I haven't seen her so relieved since—" She stopped talking abruptly.

"Since what?" I asked.

Verity shook her head. "Never mind. It's not important."

I wanted to press her but I knew that stubborn look on her face. She wasn't going to be any more forthcoming just now.

I changed the subject. "So, were there any surprises with the will?"

Verity was threading a needle. She bit off the thread and selected a little piece of lacy silk frivolity. "No, not that I could tell. The bulk of Lady E's estate went to Lord Cartwright. No surprises here."

"And Dorothy was all right." I got up to rinse my peeler free of carrot juice and sat back down to start on the swedes. "What about Peter?"

Verity quirked her mouth. "Nothing. Just a few pieces of furniture and some pictures."

I stared at her. "*Nothing*? He's inherited nothing?"

Verity shrugged. "That's what Mr Fossick said. No money."

"But—" I remembered what Verity had said about Peter coming into money. "What about the money he said he was getting?"

Verity had finished the tear in the lace of the camisole and she folded it neatly. "I don't know. Perhaps he *thought* he was going to inherit."

"Gosh." I stared blindly down at the half peeled swede in my hand. What a vindictive gesture from Lady Eveline – to reward one of her children but not the other. Had she really disliked him that much? How would that have made Peter feel?

Pushing aside that thought, I leant closer to Verity. "What else?"

Verity bit her lip, thinking. "Nothing that surprising. She didn't leave anything to Duncan, but I suppose that was to be expected – he wasn't her son, after all. Some small bequests to her sisters and a cousin. I think that was it."

"Hmm." So the principal beneficiary of Lady Eveline's will, the main inheritor of her fortune, was her husband Lord Cartwright. That was usual, I supposed. But was it another motive?

I took the vegetable peelings up to the stove and

scraped them into the stockpot which was always kept on one of the back burners at a slow simmer. I thought about Lord Cartwright and his money. I knew he was an industrialist – he'd made a lot of his fortune in manufacturing in the North of England. Had he also inherited money from his first wife?

I remembered overhearing a conversation between Mrs Anstells and Mr Fenwick, some months ago, which hadn't made much sense at the time but now did. Mrs Anstells had said something about "the speed of the wedding had seemed rather indelicate," and Mr Fenwick had admonished her in his ponderous way. "It's not for us to judge, Mrs Anstells." I'd known they were talking about the family, but now I realised they'd been talking about Lady Eveline and Lord Cartwright. Had they married quickly, after the death of the first Lady Cartwright? I decided I would ask Verity, but when I turned around, she was making her way out of the door, her arms piled with clothes and jewellery boxes. Never mind, it could wait until later.

Lunch was finished, served up and the servants' more modest repast prepared. I sat down at the table for our luncheon with a thankful sigh. The small of my back and the soles of my feet were killing me.

I noticed Nora wasn't eating much. She still looked pale. I leant over to murmur, "Are you feeling quite well?" in her ear.

She looked at me, startled, as if her thoughts

had been far away. "I'm fine, thank you, Joan," she said after a moment and flashed me a smile that was somehow dismissive.

Mentally shrugging, I turned back to my lamb stew. After lunch, I had a lovely two whole hours free before the onslaught of the evening meal preparation began. It would be a big meal tonight, with all of the family present, plus Dorothy's beau, Simon Snailer. I knew Mrs Watling was planning some elaborate centrepiece for the main course, which would no doubt involve hours of tricky, fiddly work, sweating from the heat of the stove. Oh well. I pushed the thought away and scraped the last bit of gravy from my plate. It made me remember the first place I'd ever worked, when I was just a girl recently released from the orphanage, the one with the skinflint cook. At that place, during the servants' meal, you learned to eat quickly because once the housekeeper and the butler had finished what was on their plates, that was it – the meal was over for the rest of us, regardless if you'd actually finished eating or not. The memory of it still made me cross. I got up to put my plate in the scullery sink, thanking my stars that I was working here now and not there, murder or no murder.

It was a lovely autumn day, warm for the time of year, and as it had been fairly dry that week, I decided to chance a walk, hoping the woodland paths wouldn't be too muddy. I put on my coat, affixed my hat to my head, and took up my gloves. As I walked up the kitchen stairs into the courtyard, I took a quick look at the iron clock that hung on the gable of the stable block. At least an hour, then, before I had to head back. I strode off towards the woodlands that stood at the back of the estate, determined to enjoy my short escape.

The woods were of mainly deciduous trees: oak, beech, hazel and elm. It made for pleasant walking, with the light slanting down through the bare branches and dappling the leaf-strewn walking paths. As I had hoped, it wasn't too muddy as yet, and the fallen leaves soaked up the worst of the damp. As I walked along, enjoying the rich smells of ferment and fresh air, and the distant farmyard waft of cattle and sheep, I thought back to Asharton Manor and how different it had felt, walking in the pine woods behind that huge old house. Even now, I couldn't recall the clearing, where the ancient rites of Asharte had once been performed, without a shiver.

I kept an eye on the position of the sun in relation to me as I walked, and when I judged I had about forty minutes to return to the house to be in plenty of time, I turned back. I had just opened the gate that led into the gardens of the lodge and turned the sharp corner of the path when I almost ran into the tall, dark figure of Inspector Marks.

I may have squeaked in surprise. "I'm so sorry,

sir, I do apologise, I – I didn't know you were there," I stammered.

He didn't seem perturbed. "That's no trouble, Miss Hart. Been out for a walk, I see?"

I composed myself a little. "Yes, sir. I like to walk when I have the opportunity."

"Quite right." He spoke rather absently. I looked at him more closely, and I could detect an air of – was it sadness? No, something less than that but still a negative emotion. Frustration? Annoyance?

This should have been the right time to curtsey and excuse myself. Instead, I screwed up my courage and asked "May I ask if you are any further forward with the case, sir?"

Was that too bold? I knew it was something someone like Dorothy, for example, would have no hesitation in asking. But was it really my place to enquire?

The inspector didn't seem angry. He gave me a sharp glance from under his heavy black brows. "Servants still got the wind up about an escaped lunatic, is that it?"

"Well, sir, it's not a very nice thought, is it? To think that there's somebody out there capable of doing that harm to a fellow human being."

Again, I got that glance that I'd received the first time he'd interviewed me. It was a glance of something more like respect – as if he suddenly *saw* me as a person, a real person, rather than just an anonymous face in a uniform. The warmth of it went through me like a glass of brandy.

"Miss Hart—" He stopped talking, regarding me for another moment. Then, as if on impulse, he took my arm and drew me further down the path, off into a little alcove formed by two dark yew bushes. Here we were sheltered a little from anyone's view of the path.

I was half startled, half uneasy, and that must have shown in my face.

"Forgive me, miss, but there's something I need to ask you." He leant forward a little and lowered his voice. "I know servants see everything. They might even know something, something they think is quite inconsequential, but that might have a real bearing on the outcome of a criminal case. *Think*, Joan." I was a little taken aback at his use of my first name. "Think. Is there anything that you've seen, or heard, or that your fellow workers might have seen or heard that has – shall we say – given you pause? Made you uneasy? Anything at all?"

I stared at him, my heart thumping. "I'm not often above stairs," I said stupidly.

He let go of my arm and moved away a little. I got the impression my answer had disappointed him and for a moment, I couldn't bear it, it was as if I'd sunk back in his estimation. "Wait," I said, closing the small gap between us. "Sir, if I may, I do have – I think I do have something you might think is important."

I fell silent. I'd said that bit on impulse but now it came to the meat of the story, I was nervous. Would he think I was completely indelicate? It wasn't really as if I had anything concrete to say.

Inspector Marks's attention was once more riveted on me. "Go on," he said, underlining his remark with an inclination of his head.

I swallowed. Now I came to say it, it sounded so...so thin. "Well, sir, it's probably nothing. But about three days after the – after the incident, I was just getting some kitchen things from the cupboard by the study..."

I told him honestly, and without embellishment, everything that I had overheard, such as it was. His face was impassive as I told him and I couldn't help but wonder whether he was inwardly chastising me for eavesdropping or for having indelicate ideas about my employer. "It's most probably nothing," I finished, miserably. "But I just thought I ought to tell you."

"Hmm." The inspector regarded me for a moment. "Has there been a lot of gossip about this in the servants' hall?"

"Well, not from me, sir," I said, a little spiritedly. "It may not sound like it, but I am not a gossip. The only person I've even mentioned it to is Miss Hunter."

"Hmm," the inspector said again. "Well, thank you, Miss Hart. It's certainly something we shall make a note of."

I wanted to ask whether he knew that Dorothy had been frightened about being cut out of her mother's will because of her romance with Simon Snailer but I didn't quite dare. After a moment, I became conscious of the time. I really had to get back.

"Excuse me, sir, but I must return to the kitchen – if there's nothing else I can help you with?"

"No, no, that's fine. Run along." Again, he spoke absently. I couldn't tell whether he was annoyed or intrigued by what I had told him.

"Thank you, sir. I'll say goodbye then."

I had turned to go and was about five yards away when a shout from the inspector stopped me. Startled, I turned around again.

"Joan Hart," he said, half smiling. "I *thought* I recognised the name. It was when you mentioned Miss Hunter in connection with yourself."

"Sir?"

The inspector eyed me. "Asharton Manor," was all he said.

The shock was clearly reflected on my face. I didn't know what to say.

The inspector took a few steps closer. "You and Miss Hunter had to give evidence in that trial, didn't you?"

Scarlet-faced, I nodded.

"Yes, I remember now. Impressed the judge, didn't you both? He mentioned your courage and your quick thinking in his summing up before pronouncing sentence."

An image of the hangman's noose flashed once more into my head. Out loud, I said, with what I hoped was some dignity, "Yes sir, both Verity – Miss Hunter – and myself were involved." I looked him in the eye. "It was quite a distressing experience for both of us."

"I'm sure." He looked hard at me for a moment longer and then took a step back, dismissing me. "Run along then, Miss Hart."

Chapter Thirteen

I GOT BACK TO THE KITCHEN with about thirty seconds to spare, whisked on an apron and was industrially chopping onions by the time Mrs Watling came through from her sitting room. "Gird up your loins, my girl," she said as she bustled past me and towards the stove. "It'll be a circus tonight, and no mistake."

She had her 'book' under her arm – something that all good cooks made use of. Every recipe, every little twist, every time saving trick was noted down in a notebook and taken from job to job. It was every cook's own personal bible, library and diary, rolled into one, and seeing Mrs Watling's book under her arm made me realise, rather guiltily, that recently I seemed to spend more time scribbling in my writing and storytelling notebooks than I had in my cook's book. As I transferred the sliced onions to the hot oil in the frying pan, listening with satisfaction to the sizzle, I made a mental note to update my cook's book that evening, if I had the time.

As the evening wore on, I realised how unlikely that would be. With six courses to prepare for six people, plus the servants' evening meal, there was no time to do anything but rush around from table-top to stove, from refrigerator to sink, from pantry to larder. Scarlet-faced in the steam, I chopped and boiled, mashed and rinsed, chopped some more and stirred, carried and fetched.

I was too busy to be aware of much else around me other than the job in hand. Even so, the first time Nora came into the kitchen in search of a clean apron – she was waiting at table tonight – I had to take another look. She looked as pale as milk. As she came into the kitchen, walking through the hot, heavy, food-scented air, I saw her swallow and her pallor increased to an extent that was almost alarming.

"Nora." I put the saucepan I was carrying down and stepped smartly over to her, catching her by the arm. For a moment I thought she was going to faint. "Are you all right?"

I drew her over to the back door and onto the bottom step of the flight that led up to the courtyard. The cold night air seemed to revive her a little

"Gosh, thank you Joan." She took a deep breath and then another. "I just – I felt rather sick. I think it was just the heat."

I looked at her hard. "You've not looked well all day. Is there something wrong?"

For a moment, she looked frightened. I could see her making up her mind as to whether to confide in me but then there was a shout from Mrs Watling and I made a sound of annoyance. "Look, I've got to go. Stay out here for a bit, get some air."

Nora nodded thankfully. I hurried back to the chaos of the kitchen.

"Those potatoes are going to be mush, Joan," gasped Mrs Watling as she hurried past me with the sirloin of beef. "Come on, look lively."

"Sorry. Nora was ill—" It was pointless saying any more. I knew Mrs Watling was a good sort, it was just that this part of the job meant she had to snap and shout. Every dish that went up to the table up there was a reflection of the cook's skill and efficiency, and every day could be the day when something went wrong.

Somehow, we all got through the evening. At about half-past ten, when the tray of coffee, the cheeseboard, and the fruit and savoury biscuits had been carried up, Mrs Watling and I collapsed into the two chairs in her sitting room, too tired even to think about making tea.

"Good Lord, I'm getting too old for this," Mrs Watling murmured. I murmured something non-committal back. For a moment, I had a qualm about the future, not something I normally allowed myself to think about too much. I had ambition, definitely, but would that ever come to fruition? Or would I just end up working as a skivvy for the rest of my life, until I got too old to do it anymore and then...what? Would there still be workhouses in the future? What would happen to me?

Shaking my head to dispel these gloomy thoughts, I forced myself to sit up.

"Joan, be a good girl and pour me a small sherry." Mrs Watling stared up at the low ceiling of her room, her eyes stretched wide. I knew that feeling. You kept your eyes open because if you shut them, even for a few moments, you would fall asleep.

"Of course." Feeling pity for her and for myself, I heaved myself to my feet and staggered through to the kitchen. I was surprised to see Verity walking through the doorway, her face anxious. "Hello, V. What's wrong?" For some reason, I had a jump of paranoia that we, the kitchen staff, had messed up the food.

Verity tried to smile. "Don't worry, Joan, it's nothing you've done." She had an uncanny knack of reading my mind, sometimes. "No, it's just they've all just had a big row. Upstairs."

"Upstairs? The family have?"

Verity nodded. She sat down at the kitchen table and propped her pointy chin on her hands. "Dorothy told me about it when she came up to her room. Apparently Peter wasn't there tonight and he should have been. Lord C got really angry because apparently, the police want to talk to him again."

"Talk to who?"

"The police want to talk to Peter again."

"Oh." I reached for three sherry glasses and poured a generous tot of sherry into each one. Then I slid one across the table to Verity. "Here. You have one too. I'll just take this through to Mrs Watling."

When I got back, Verity had drained the glass and was wiping her lips with the back of her hand like a thirsty sailor. "That hit the spot, Joan. Thank you."

"You're welcome." I sat down opposite her with my own glass. "So where was Peter, then?"

Verity shrugged. "No idea. He just didn't turn up for dinner."

"No wonder Lord C was cross."

"It wasn't just that. He made some rude remark about Simon Snailer. Then Dorothy blew up, and then *they* had a shouting match." Verity shook her head. "Duncan pulled Dorothy up for being rude to his father, then Dorothy had a go back at him. What a mess."

I couldn't help but giggle at the image of all these supposedly high-born, well-bred people brawling like dock-workers. Verity smiled tiredly as well. "I know, Joan. The footmen and Mr Fenwick must have got a right earful."

I had wondered why so much of our beautifully made dinner had come back down almost untouched. They must have all been too busy shouting to eat much. I tried to feel cross at all that hard work going to waste, but I was just too tired.

Verity yawned. She braced her hands against the table and stood up. "Anyway, I just came down to get a hot chocolate for Dorothy. She's having an early night for once, thank the Lord, up there in her room turning the air blue. She's still absolutely *steaming*."

"Take her a sherry," I suggested, giggling a little.

Verity gave me a wry look. "She's had far too much already. Hot chocolate it will have to be."

I let her make the hot chocolate for once – I didn't want to even touch the stove again after the evening's work. Verity was just leaving the room when something occurred to me. I called her back.

"What is it, Joan?"

"It's Nora," I said. "She's not been herself lately, have you noticed? She came in this evening and I thought she was going to drop."

Verity looked worried again. "Now you mention it – she was sick the other morning. I was waiting outside the bathroom and I could hear her."

We both looked at one another, the penny dropping. Verity looked stricken.

"Bloody hell," she swore. "She can't be—"

We were silent for a moment. I put my hand up to my mouth. "We might be wrong," I suggested, somewhat feebly.

"God, Joanie, I hope so. Oh Lord..." Verity trailed off. "We'd better ask her," she suggested.

I nodded, feeling grim at the very thought. "All right. But, let's pick the moment, shall we? She might not even want to tell us if we gang up on her."

"No, you're right." Verity briefly closed her eyes. "Bloody hell, this is all we need." She gave me a quick squeeze of the arm. "I'd better go. Talk to you later."

I finished my sherry, glad of the warmth that spread down my throat as I swallowed it. I wondered whether Peter Drew's absence had anything to do with what I'd told Inspector Marks in the garden that afternoon. But how could it? My thoughts slipped from Peter Drew to Nora. What if Nora was pregnant? I washed up my sherry glass, feeling cold with empathic dread.

It was another hour before the kitchen was ship-shape, and by then I was almost asleep on my feet. I hung the last shining copper saucepan back on its hook, gave the table a final wipe, rinsed and hung the cloth over the sink tap and stood back, surveying the room. So much for having time to write up my book. I would be lucky to make it to bed before collapsing. I sighed and turned for the door, dreading the long climb upstairs to my bed.

Chapter Fourteen

I WOKE THE NEXT MORNING TO hear the sound of heavy rain. Although it was dark and cold as usual, the patter of raindrops on the eaves above me made a cosy sort of sound. I groped for the matchbox, lit the lamp and felt for my slippers, my toes curling away from the cold linoleum. Verity was a gently breathing heap curled under the bedclothes. I made sure her feet were tucked beneath the blankets and tiptoed out of the room.

I washed, dressed and went to rouse Maggie. Together we trooped down the servants' stairs, yawning and not saying much to one another. Maggie went to fill the kettle, and I rubbed the sleep out of my eyes and went to have a look at what was on the menu for today. We followed a fortnightly pattern; mostly the same dishes on rotation, changing over every two weeks, unless the family had company or were otherwise entertaining. It made preparation and food ordering much easier.

I didn't mind cooking breakfast. It was always

the same, and by now I could almost do it in my sleep (which was handy some mornings, I can tell you). The main challenge was getting everything prepared at the same time so it could be carried up to the sideboard in the dining table for the family to help themselves. It was the one meal of the day where they weren't waited on.

I'd forgotten about Nora in the rush of the morning but as we all sat down to breakfast, I caught Verity's eye across the table and she inclined her head very slightly to indicate where Nora was sitting, three chairs down. Immediately recalling what we'd spoken about, I looked and my heart sank. Nora still looked dreadful; ashy pale, with great half-moons of shadow beneath her eyes. She had only eaten a miniscule bit of porridge. I looked back at Verity and shook my head very slightly. We would have to wait for the right moment to confront poor Nora. I found myself hoping quite desperately that Nora actually had some dreadful but quite innocent illness that mimicked all the symptoms of pregnancy.

The lunch for the day was a lighter one, thankfully: vegetable soup, Dover sole with accompaniments, lemon tart and cream. I reached for a chopping board and handed it to Maggie. "We may as well get the soup started now. Be a good girl and chop up some swede and carrot, will you? I'll do the onions."

Maggie took the board. Rooting around in the vegetable rack, she looked up at me from her kneeling position. "We're out of swedes."

"Well, go and get some more, then." Honestly. Maggie was a nice girl but she didn't have much *initiative*. She nodded obediently and went off in the direction of the root cellar.

Mrs Watling was already making up the batter for the Dover sole. "I wonder if they'll all be sitting up to table again tonight?" she mused. I shrugged. No doubt Miss Rosalind would be down to consult with us, lording it over us as if she were the lady of the manor.

I'd just begun on the onions when there was a scream so violent that I jumped and the knife flew out of my hand and fell to the floor, missing my foot by an inch.

"Good God, what was that?" Mrs Watling froze by the stove, her hand up to her chest. "What was that?"

The screaming continued. Shaking, I rushed towards where the sound was coming from. As I got closer to the cellar steps, I could hear better, and I realised it was Maggie who was screaming.

The footman, Andrew, was right behind me, running, his face set. Together we almost fell down the cellar steps in our haste to reach Maggie. Even in the dim light of the cellar, I could see her standing up where the passageway turned a corner into the darkest part of the room. Her hands were buried in her hair and her mouth was an open hole.

"What is it? What's the matter?" I gasped, skidding to a stop. Andrew ran past both of us, round the corner. I heard him gasp.

"What is it? What is it?" I asked, terrified. Maggie cast herself into my arms, weeping and gulping.

Andrew came back into view, white and shaking. "Don't go back there, Joan," he warned, his teeth chattering. Then he said a very bad word.

"What is it?" I don't know why I kept asking the same things. It wasn't as if anyone was answering me.

I could hear other hurrying footsteps up above and then thundering down the cellar steps. Verity, Albert, Nora and Mrs Watling came running up to us. They all started talking at once.

I thrust Maggie at Mrs Watling and strode around the corner. "Don't, Joan!" Andrew said again, making a grab for me, but I jigged aside, escaping him. I already had an inkling of what it was I was going to see, but the actual sight of it stopped me dead in my tracks.

I stood, hugging my arms across my trembling body, looking at the dead body of Peter Drew. As I stood there, silent and aghast, Verity came up beside me. I heard her gasp but she didn't say anything else. We both stood looking down at him.

He looked as though he'd been dead for some time, and even in the dim light, I could see the brownish stains on his shirt-front.

After what seemed like hours, but was probably only a few minutes, Verity took me by the arm, propelled me round, and steered me back around the corner. Andrew had already disappeared, no doubt to warn Mr Fenwick to call the police. Maggie was being shepherded up the stairs, supported on either side by Mrs Watling and Nora.

"Come on," Verity said sharply to Albert, who looked as though he were about to go and look himself. "We have to clear this room for the police."

"What is it?" His eyes were like saucers.

Verity grabbed his arm with her free hand and pushed him back up the stairs. "Never you mind."

"Come on, Verity—"

"It's not your business."

He was still arguing with her when he got back to the kitchen. I don't know why she wouldn't tell him – it wasn't as if it was going to be a secret.

Albert shook off Verity's hand and ran off in the direction of the hallway. I knew he'd gone to find Andrew, to see if he would tell him what was happening.

"Sit down, Joan," Verity said, almost pushing me into a chair. I subsided gratefully, realising I was actually feeling a bit light-headed. Verity sat down opposite me, and we stared at each other across the table, wide-eyed and silent.

IT WAS LIKE SOME AWFUL deja-vu that day. Again, the police cars came crunching over the gravel driveway, parking with a screech of brakes. Again, Mr Fenwick ponderously showed them through to the family. Again, Verity had to tend to Dorothy who was in bed having hysterics. Mrs Watling and I prepared possibly the worst meal we'd ever made, managing to burn both the meat and vegetables, dropping the prepared pudding on the floor. We looked at one another in despair before I bent down to pick up the broken pieces of china and scrape up the fruit and cream from the red tiles.

"I can't send that up," said Mrs Watling in a shaky voice. She sat down at the table and put her head in her hands. I patted her on the shoulder, not knowing what else to do.

"Nobody's going to eat anything, anyway," Maggie said in a watery voice. She'd done nothing all morning but sit hunched over in one of Mrs Watling's armchairs, which had been brought through from her sitting room.

At that moment, there was a heavy step on the stairs outside and a moment later, Inspector Marks walked into the kitchen, frowning. Mrs Watling,

Maggie and I all looked at him in a sort of glazed silence.

"Peter Drew has been murdered, as I'm sure you ladies are aware," Inspector Marks said sternly. "Miss Langton—" He turned directly to Maggie. "I understand you found the body?"

Maggie gulped and nodded. "Then I'll need to speak to you right away," said the inspector.

Mrs Watling cleared her throat. "Inspector, would you mind if myself or Joan sat in on that interview? Maggie is very young."

The inspector frowned. Then he turned to me. "Miss Hart, I understand you were quickly on the scene when your colleague here screamed?" I nodded. The inspector continued. "Then you can accompany your colleague. I also have some questions for you."

"You can use my sitting room," Mrs Watling said tiredly. She looked as if she didn't have the strength to rise from her chair.

The inspector ushered us through to the room ahead of him. I held Maggie's arm and steered her in the direction of a spare chair. There wasn't one for me and the inspector so I remained standing.

"Sit down, Miss Hart," said Inspector Marks. I blushed and did so. He propped himself up against the edge of Mrs Watling's sideboard.

"Now, Miss Langton. What happened this morning? Why were you in the cellar?"

Maggie gulped. "I was just getting some vegetables, sir. We'd run out and we needed them for the soup." She stopped abruptly.

"Go on, please."

I was too far away to give her a nudge but I sent an expressive look across the room. Her eyes flickered to mine and she sat up a little. "I don't know what else to say, sir. I was just getting the swedes, and I went around the corner to where they were, and I – I saw him."

"Did you touch anything?"

Maggie looked confused. "No. I don't think so."

The inspector looked over at me. "What about you, Miss Hart?"

"Of course not," I said, rather more sharply than I'd intended.

"Hmm." The inspector regarded me from under lowered brows for a moment. Then he said, "No, I expect you wouldn't have done such a thing." Maggie looked even more confused. "Why were you there, Miss Hart?"

"Because I heard Maggie screaming." I could feel myself becoming a little annoyed. Perhaps it was the shock, hitting me at last. "I heard my colleague screaming, so of course I ran to help. Andrew – Mr Collier, the first footman, I mean – did too. He also saw the body."

"I've already interviewed Mr Collier." The inspector re-crossed his ankles and settled himself back again. "Now, when was the last time you were in the cellar? Before this morning, I mean."

I thought back. "It must have been several days ago."

"Did you go as far into the room as Maggie went this morning? I mean, did you see anything suspicious?"

I shook my head, sure of that point. "No, sir. Nothing that was at all untoward."

The inspector looked at me for another moment, rubbing his moustache. Then he nodded. "We're still establishing a time of death," he said after a moment. "So any information you could give me would be helpful. Can you and Miss Langton tell me the last time you saw the deceased, Peter Drew?"

I was silent, thinking. Maggie tentatively raised her hand. "I haven't seen him for over a week, sir. I don't leave the kitchens much."

"Thank you. Miss Hart?"

Suddenly, it came to me where I had seen Peter Drew last. He'd been in Duncan Cartwright's bedroom, sneaking out of the door. I wanted to tell the inspector, but I didn't want to say anything in front of Maggie.

I didn't have the nerve to ask her to leave, not when we were both there on Inspector Marks's say-so. Instead I inclined my head very slightly towards her, holding the inspector's gaze, and raised my eyebrows. Would he understand?

He did, thankfully. "Thank you, Miss Langton, I think that will be all now. You may return to your duties." Maggie got up and scuttled out of the room, her shoulders dropping with relief. Then he turned to me. "You have some information, Miss Hart?"

I nodded. "It may be nothing of course—" I went on to tell him everything I had seen. I even included the anecdote about the butler at the house I'd worked at previously, who'd been brought back to mind with Peter's actions.

"Thank you, Miss Hart," Inspector Marks said once I'd finished. He said it in a neutral way but I was beginning to understand that he spoke like that when he'd heard something that excited him. He didn't want to show it but I was pretty sure that my little piece of information had been important, after all.

In the short silence that followed, I screwed up my nerve. "Sir, may I – may I ask how poor Mr Drew died?"

For a moment, I thought he wouldn't answer me. Then he said, rather absently, "The post mortem hasn't yet been conducted so we don't know – officially."

"But, unofficially?" I asked, greatly daring.

The inspector smiled. "If I didn't know better, Miss Hart, I'd believe you harbour ambitions to become a police officer."

I was shocked. A female police officer? Of course,

I knew in theory they existed but I'd never seen one. Besides, it wasn't really that I was interested in police work – I was interested in solving the mystery.

"I think I'd rather be a detective, sir," I said, so boldly I surprised myself.

The inspector laughed. Then he saw my face and his laughter died. "Forgive me, Miss Hart. You surprised me, that's all." He looked at me appraisingly. "You *are* quite surprising, Miss Hart. For what it's worth, I think you're wasted as a cook."

"I'm only the undercook," I said, stupidly. I was so taken aback by what he'd said it was all I could think of to say.

The inspector smiled. "Well, the world is changing, Miss Hart. Who knows what opportunities there will be for bright young women in the future?" He rubbed his moustache again and then stood up. "And now, I must get on with my work. Thank you for the information."

Knowing a dismissal when I heard one, I stood up too and bobbed a curtsey. "Thank you, sir," was an inadequate goodbye but it would have to do.

Again, I was walking away when he called me back. I turned, eagerly.

"Miss Hart, you haven't worked here very long, have you?"

Nonplussed, I shook my head. "Only six months or so, sir."

"So you never worked for the family in their London house?"

"No, that's correct, sir. But of course, I will do when the family returns to London for the season."

The inspector nodded but he had a funny look on his face, as if he were thinking that perhaps that would never happen. Then he asked "Your friend, Miss Hunter, she's worked for them for some years, yes?"

"Yes, about eight years, sir."

"She was working for them in London when the first Lady Cartwright died?"

"Yes, sir," I said, puzzled.

"Right," said the inspector. Then he suddenly became brisk. "Thank you, Miss Hart. You can go now."

Chapter Fifteen

I WAS ALMOST DEAD ON MY feet by the end of the day, but I willed myself to stay awake once I got back to Verity's and my room. I had to talk to Verity, no matter how tired I was. Whether that meant waiting up until she could leave Dorothy at three o'clock in the morning, for example, then so be it. I'd supplied myself by sneaking up a full teapot and some biscuits, which I then hid under the bed, fortifying myself with them at intervals.

As it happened, she came in quite early. I'd checked our little alarm clock at ten and Verity came in at twenty past the hour. She sort of slumped through the doorway, her head hanging down, and sat down with a thump on her bed, staring at me with dull eyes.

"What's the matter?" I asked in alarm and then mentally shook myself. What was I even asking that sort of question?

Verity half laughed. "What a question, Joanie."

"I know. Sorry. It's been a long day."

"Don't I know it?" Verity allowed herself to fall sideways so that she was lying on the bed. "This is like living in a nightmare, Joan. It simply goes on and on." She turned her head on the pillow to look at me. "Now I know what it must have been like for you at Asharton Manor, you poor thing."

"That was different," I said honestly. "It wasn't – it wasn't brutal." Of course, I hadn't felt like that at the time, but looking back, I could see how it had been different. "This is..." I couldn't finish and the words just drifted off into silence.

I remembered I still had some tea left and got up to pour Verity a cup. I had to use my dirty teacup as I'd only managed to smuggle one up, but I knew she wouldn't mind.

"It's still fairly hot," I said, handing her the saucer.

"Oh, thank you. Just what I need." Verity took a sip and remarked "I should have swiped some of Dorothy's brandy."

"How is she?" I asked, tentatively.

Verity closed her eyes briefly and shook her head. "Not good. I had to get her to take a sleeping pill in the end. I was worried—" She stopped talking for a moment and then said, with difficulty, "I was worried she was going to hurt herself. Do something stupid. That's why I've got to be up early in the morning, before she wakes up."

"You're not her keeper, V," I said, but gently. It

must have been hard for Verity to remain detached, given her mistress's distress.

"I know. It's just – oh, Joanie, it's so awful. I know she didn't much like her brother but he *was* her brother. And having lost her mother as well, and her father..." She trailed off.

It got me thinking. Surely Dorothy could have nothing to do with these killings? *Surely*? Will or no will? I remembered how distressed she had been when the police had arrested Peter. Surely no sister or daughter could have done these things, not unless they were a deranged lunatic, and if that were the case, surely it would be obvious. Wouldn't it?

In my silence of the last few moments, Verity had heaved herself upright and begun undressing. Tiredly, she unpinned her hair and sat down in front of the mirror to brush it out.

"I can do that," I offered. I could see she had scarcely the energy to lift the brush.

"Thank you."

I drew the brush through her fine, red-gold hair, the colour of a fox pelt or of autumn leaves. Verity closed her eyes, sighing. "My mother used to do this for me," she said in a small voice.

I couldn't think of what to say, but I smiled sympathetically at her in the mirror. Then I remembered what it was I wanted to ask her. "Did the inspector talk to you?"

Verity opened her eyes. "Yes. He managed to

get me after I'd finally got Dorothy to sleep. I've only just come up from the room they're using for interviews."

"What did he want to ask you?"

Verity frowned. "Well, of course I had to say when I'd last seen Peter. And that wasn't that long ago, it was the day before yesterday. He was driving off towards the village in Dorothy's car."

"What else?" I'd worked out the last tangle, and I gently detached the brush from Verity's hair and put it back down on the dressing table.

Verity sighed. "It was strange. He wanted to know all about when I worked for the family when the first Lady C was alive. Of course, I wasn't Dorothy's lady's maid then, I was the second housemaid."

"Yes?" I prompted.

"Well, he kept asking me questions about the night she died. About what her relationship with the servants was like and with the other members of the family. How his Lordship treated her." Her gaze met mine in the mirror. "Strange, isn't it?"

I was silent, thinking. Verity got up and made her way back to her bed. She was frowning again, the smooth white skin of her forehead bunching like creased linen.

"Maybe..." I began tentatively, and then stopped. Verity looked at me. "What is it?"

I took a deep breath. "Maybe the inspector

thinks that these deaths are related to the death of the first Lady Cartwright."

We looked at one another in silence. Verity said "How could they be, Joan? That was an accident."

"Was it?" I asked.

Verity's eyes widened. "Well, of course it was. There was never any suggestion of—" She broke off abruptly.

I sat tensely. "What, V?"

Verity was staring into space, her mind obviously far away. "That's odd you said that," she said slowly after a moment. "That's odd. It's just reminded me of something strange that happened right after Lady C – the first one – died."

"What?" I asked, breathlessly.

Verity was biting her lip. "Do you remember Gladys? She was a housemaid too, she worked with me."

I thought back to my visits to the Cartwright townhouse. *Gladys, Gladys...* after a moment I managed to recall a tall girl, rather buxom. Quite a saucy manner on her but Verity had always said she was a nice girl, if a bit lazy.

"I think so," I said, slowly. "Dark hair, yes? Quite an eye for the boys?"

Verity grinned. "Yes, that was Gladys."

"What about her?"

Verity stopped grinning. "Well, that's just it. Just after the first Lady C died, Gladys gave notice.

Really soon after it happened, perhaps two days afterwards."

"And?" I prompted because she stopped speaking again.

"Well, I always thought it was funny."

I suppressed a scream with difficulty. "What was? Come on, V, spit it out."

Verity smiled sheepishly. "Sorry. I'm not trying to be mysterious, I'm just thinking. I hadn't thought about this for years but now, it's coming back to me." Just as I was thinking about bashing her over the head with a pillow to get her to come to the point, she shook her head and sat up. "This is the thing, Joan. Lady Cartwright, Alice Cartwright, fell down the stairs and died, about five years ago now. A day or so after she died, Gladys gave notice, and she left very quickly after that, about a week later. I don't even think she had a new situation to go to." She looked at me.

"Right," I said after a moment, realising I was supposed to make a contribution.

"Well," said Verity, continuing. "It was a pretty awful time, what with the accident and the police and everyone upset, so I didn't really think about Gladys leaving so quickly or so suddenly. But now I look back it's...odd. *Very* odd. Why did she just suddenly leave, for no reason?"

I was thinking. "She wasn't dismissed?"

Verity shook her head. "No, definitely not. We would have known."

I frowned. "You don't think... You don't think Gladys had anything to do with Lady Alice falling, do you?"

Verity looked shocked. "Of course not, Joan. That wasn't what I meant at all. Gladys wouldn't have hurt a fly; she would never do something as wicked as – as what you're suggesting."

"Well, what then?" I asked, rather impatiently. "I meant, do you think the accident could have been her fault but that she didn't mean to do it? I mean, could she, I don't know, have loosened the stair-rod accidentally or something like that and of course not meant to hurt anyone, but when the cause of the accident came out, Gladys was terrified she would be blamed and that's why she gave notice?"

Verity had been shaking her head slowly through this entire speech of mine. "No. No, Joan, that's not what I meant." She looked me in the eye and said "But what if she saw something? Or someone?"

Silence fell as I mulled that over. It was funny, but now Verity had made it, it didn't seem like such an outrageous suggestion. That was what living through two murders did for you. It turned you into someone who could quite easily accept that an accident had been anything but.

Eventually I spoke. "It's possible," I said slowly. I was in my own bed by this time, and I realised

I was pleating the blanket nervously between my fingers. "So, what we're really saying is, it's possible that Lady Alice's accident wasn't an accident and that there may have been a witness in Gladys?"

Verity and I looked at one another solemnly. "Yes," she said.

I fell back upon my pillows with a sigh. "Lord give me strength." I remembered the bold remark I'd made to Inspector Marks that afternoon. *I would really rather be a detective.* What a silly thing to have said. He must have thought I was a lunatic.

"Should I tell the inspector?" Verity asked.

I blew out my cheeks. "I suppose so. I don't know, though. It's not exactly evidence, is it?"

Verity slid down beneath the blankets, yawning. "Sorry, Joan, I can't stay awake any longer. Tell you what we can do, though."

"What's that?" I asked, catching the yawn. Looking at the clock, I could see it was almost midnight. We had both better get some rest.

"I'll write to Gladys. I've got her mother's address, and she'll be able to forward it on."

"You're not going to ask her – well, what we just talked about, surely?"

"Of course not, Joanie, what do you take me for? I'll just see if she wants to meet us, for you to be there as well. We can go into details when we see her. *If* we see her."

"Fine." I was so tired now I couldn't stop the

droop of my eyelids. It sounded rather a hopeless plan to me, but in the face of nothing better, I was prepared to give it a go.

"Turn off the lamp, Joanie," came Verity's voice, muffled under the covers.

I did so and lay down, sliding into darkness and unconsciousness in a matter of moments.

Chapter Sixteen

THE UPHEAVAL OF THE LAST day had driven any thought of Nora's possible predicament from my mind, and I was sure, from Verity's. It wasn't until I sat down to breakfast that I remembered. Nora was still pale, still pushing food around the bowl and not really eating it. I caught Verity's eye and nodded my head towards Nora, and Verity set her mouth and nodded.

We caught up with her after breakfast, in the hallway, as she was making her way upstairs.

"Nora," Verity hissed. Nora jumped and nearly lost her footing. She turned around and saw us both gesticulating to her.

"What's wrong?" she asked.

"Come down here a moment."

"I have to get the breakfast trays—"

"That can wait a minute," Verity said impatiently. "Come on, come in here."

We all crammed into one of the store cupboards,

where we kept the flour and sugar and rice in big stone barrels. The dusty air made me sneeze.

"What's wrong?" Nora asked, looking scared. It occurred to me that she might think it was something to do with the murder.

Verity took a deep breath. "Nora..." She trailed away and looked at me, as if for inspiration. I nodded encouragingly. "Nora, it's hard to ask this but are you – are you in trouble?"

Nora said nothing but her pallor was eclipsed by a rosy red flush that rose to her eyebrows. She opened her mouth to say something and then abruptly burst into tears.

We crowded around her, clucking and petting her like a child. "It's fine, it's fine," soothed Verity. "You can tell us. Don't worry."

Nora raised a tear-stained face. "You can't tell anybody," she whispered, fiercely. "God help me, I don't know what to do."

Verity looked stricken. "You're sure, then?"

Nora nodded miserably. I didn't say anything – what was there to say? I just stood there in the cramped cupboard, feeling helpless.

Nora was sobbing quietly. "They'll turn me out without a reference and then where will I go? No one will take me on, I'll never be able to get a job."

Verity's face was creased up with sympathetic anguish. "Could you go home?"

Nora shook her head, scattering tears. One

hit my lip and I tasted salt. "I can't – I just can't! The shame would kill my mother – and they've got too many to feed as it is. Dad can't work anymore because of his lungs..." Her voice thickened with tears and it was hard to understand what she was saying.

At the sound of voices in the corridor outside the closed door we all froze. Silently, we stood there as if turned into stone, until the voices – it sounded like Mr Fenwick and Mrs Anstells – moved further away down the corridor.

"Okay, we can't talk about it any more, here and now," Verity whispered. "But Nora, don't worry. We'll sort something out. We'll see you right. Very well? You're not to worry?"

I couldn't see Nora adhering to this command very strictly, but she nodded all the same. "Please, please don't tell anyone."

I found my voice. "We won't, Nora, we absolutely promise." I looked across at Verity, and she nodded fervently.

"Of course we won't," she said.

"Come on," I murmured. "Let's go while there's nobody around." I gave Nora a quick, friendly squeeze of the arm. "Don't worry, Nora. I'm sure there's something to be done."

She gave us both a grateful, if watery, smile. Then we hurried out of the cupboard, one by one, listening out for approaching footsteps and quickly going our separate ways.

I went back to the kitchen and started the preparations for lunch in something of a dream. A small prudish part of me was shocked – I'll admit it. I couldn't imagine taking the *risk* that Nora had. A second thought struck me. Who was the father? I stood still for a moment, staring into space, my hands full of mushrooms. I tried to remember if I'd ever seen any of the male servants paying special attention to Nora. Well, of course, they all had – she was a very pretty, lively girl. But, thinking back, had there been anyone paying her *particular* attention?

"Joan, come on. Stop wool-gathering." Mrs Watling swept past with a brimming pot and made me jump. "I know we're all at sixes and sevens at the moment, things being what they are, but we can't all go to pieces."

"Sorry," I muttered, returning to my task. As I wiped and chopped the mushrooms, I tried not to think any more about Nora, Nora and her possible suitors. It seemed slightly indelicate and I was a little ashamed of myself for being so curious.

The half-pound of mushrooms were chopped and ready. I mixed the *roux* of butter, milk and flour together and began to heat it slowly on the stove. Chicken stock, lemon juice, pepper, salt and tip in the mushrooms...there was something soothing about making soup. Soothing was what I needed right then.

Just as I was standing there, stirring the gradually thickening soup, my blasted imagination started working again. Try as I might, my thoughts returned first to Nora and then to the most recent murder. I blinked against the mushroom-scented steam. An appalling thought suddenly sprang into my head.

I clutched the wooden spoon, trying to tell myself not to be so silly. But the thought would not budge. What if – what if Peter had been the father of Nora's baby? What if she'd gone to him for help and he'd laughed or spurned her in some way and she'd lost her temper and – and killed him?

You're being ridiculous, I told myself, stirring fiercely. Yes, Nora had a temper, that was true. I suppose being with child could make you act irrationally at times. But surely, *surely* she wouldn't have done such a violent, wicked thing? Your imagination is running away with you, I told myself sternly. Just stop being so silly and get back to work.

I made a giant effort to start thinking about something else, anything else. I concentrated on the fish course; crab fishcakes covered in breadcrumbs, served with a fresh tartar sauce. As I chopped and peeled and fried, I kept my mind resolutely away from thoughts of pregnancy and murder.

It worked – until lunchtime, when we all sat

down for our hasty meal. Nora sat next to Verity, as normal, but she didn't speak to either of us. Indeed, she seemed to be avoiding our gaze as much as possible. I sympathised, I supposed she was embarrassed. *Poor girl.* I stopped trying to attract her attention and focused my gaze on my cold tongue sandwich.

The servants' grapevine was in fine working order that morning, I can tell you. By the end of the meal, despite Mr Fenwick's admonishments, we all knew who upstairs had an alibi and who was in the clear for Peter Drew's murder.

"That Duncan, he was off at his club all the evening when they say Mr Drew was killed, so he's out," Maggie said, her eyes like saucers. "And Miss Dorothy don't have a leg to stand on. She was in her room all evening, but nobody except Verity saw her, and that was only for a few hours here and there."

"Really," I said, a little annoyed. Much as Dorothy was lazy and spoilt, I just couldn't see her knifing her own brother to death or bashing her own mother over the head. So alibi or no alibi, how could she have done it? And why? No, despite her bad points, Dorothy was no murderer. I was sure of that.

Verity drew me aside as we took our plates into the scullery. "Did you know that Lord C and Rosalind had alibied themselves again?"

"Again?" I put my plate on top of the stack and flashed Maggie, who was standing armed and ready at the sink, a sympathetic smile. "What, were they 'working late' in the office again?"

Verity smirked. "Apparently."

I rolled my eyes. "I see."

We walked together towards the corridor.

"Listen," Verity said. "I've got to go back up to Dorothy. I don't want to leave her alone at the moment."

"I understand."

Verity leaned in a little closer. "What are we going to do about Nora?"

I stopped walking for a moment. Verity tugged me forward. "I don't know," I confessed. "Will she even let us help her? You saw what she was like at luncheon."

"She's embarrassed," Verity said. "And she's terrified. No, I've been thinking it over."

"And?"

Verity looked thoughtful. "Well, there are two possibilities. Perhaps more than two."

"What's the first?" By now we had reached the foot of the stairs and I was worried about being overheard.

"That's the final option," Verity said, somewhat mysteriously. "We could try something else first."

"Like what?" I thought back to all those muttered, whispered, underhand conversations that went around from girl to girl, from woman to woman. "Mustard baths? Carrying something heavy?"

"That's a good start. We could try gin."

173

"Oh, V." I looked at her, exasperated. "How are we going to afford to buy gin?"

Verity set her chin. "If it comes to that," she said quietly but mulishly, "I'll steal some."

"Shh!" I glanced around, terrified someone would hear her. "Listen, I know Nora's nice, and she's a friend, but there's no need for you to get into trouble over what's happened to her."

I could hear footsteps behind us, coming up the corridor. Oh, for a place to talk where one wasn't constantly interrupted! "Listen, you'd better go. We'll talk later."

"Of course." Verity squeezed my arm. "It'll be all right, I'm sure. We'll manage."

I watched her run lightly up the stairs and around the corner out of sight. Mrs Anstells appeared at my shoulder. "Don't you have somewhere to be, Joan?"

"Yes, I'm sorry." I braced myself for a scolding but to my surprise she gave me quite a sympathetic smile.

"It's not an easy time, my dear. I appreciate how you've managed to keep up to your usual high standards of work. Of course, Mrs Watling runs a tight ship but – there you go."

I flushed, pleased at the praise. Then I nodded my head in a respectful way and made my way back to the kitchen.

Chapter Seventeen

ROSALIND MAKEPEACE HADN'T BEEN SEEN in the kitchens since Peter Drew's body was discovered. I'd supposed she'd been too busy dealing with Lord Cartwright and the police and so forth to bother coming down here to boss me and Mrs Watling about and let us know just what we were doing wrong. Talk of the devil – she came down that evening after dinner in search of Mrs Anstells. Maggie and I were busy putting away the saucepans and dishes, and it was some time before I noticed Rosalind standing in the kitchen, staring at us as if we were something you'd find in the zoo.

As soon as I'd got to my feet and taken a proper look at her, I was ashamed of my previous thought. She looked dreadful, drawn and pale and with such shadows under her eyes they almost matched the black of her hair. She'd always been neatly turned out – not exactly fashionably dressed, not like Dorothy – but she'd always been so clean and neat and polished it was as if she'd been made in a factory somewhere, shiny and new. Now, she wore an old sweater I'd not seen before, in a shade of muddy blue that did nothing for her complexion, and an old tweed skirt that looked as though she'd dug it out of a pre-War fashion collection.

"Can I help you, Miss?" I asked, trying to sound as respectful as possible.

"I was looking for Mrs Anstells," she said, faintly, after a moment.

"I believe she's talking to Mrs Watling," I said. "Shall I call for her?"

Rosalind stared at me while I spoke. I had the odd impression she didn't really see me. It was as if she could hear me talking but not see where the sound was coming from. The back of my neck prickled.

She was silent for so long that I almost repeated myself, and then she said quietly, "No, don't bother. I'll go through myself."

She walked through the kitchen so quietly it was almost as if she were a ghost. Both Maggie and I rotated to watch her go – we couldn't help it, it was so eerie.

"What's wrong with her?" whispered Maggie.

I shrugged. "She's probably under an awful lot of strain." For the first time, I realised this was probably true and felt a flicker of sympathy for her. "She's got to keep his Lordship happy, deal with

Duncan and basically run everything with no help from anyone else."

Rosalind didn't come back through the kitchen. I supposed she'd sat down with Mrs Anstells and Mrs Watling in Mrs Watling's sitting room. I sent Maggie off upstairs while I did a last check of the room and gave the kitchen table one last wipe. Everything was in order for tomorrow. I resisted an ignoble impulse to go and listen at Mrs Watling's door and forced myself to leave the room.

After the long and weary climb up the back stairs, I entered our room to find Verity already there, unlacing her shoes and rubbing her feet.

"They can't hurt worse than mine," I remarked, flopping gratefully onto my bed.

"No, probably not." Verity straightened up, sighing. "Lord, what a day."

"How is Dorothy?"

Verity became immediately serious. "She's saying she wants to leave this place. She wants to go to London."

My stomach dropped. "Really?"

Verity nodded. "She'll have to get permission from the inspector, first. I can't imagine he's going to want anyone to leave until – until they arrest somebody."

I started to breathe again. "Yes, I suppose you're right." I bent and began removing my own shoes, noting with annoyance that the heel of my right shoe was coming slightly loose. More expense.

Verity began to unbutton her black dress. "If I know Dorothy, she'll manage to persuade him."

"So that would mean you'd go with her? Is that correct?"

Verity nodded. She must have noticed the dismay on my face. "Don't fret, Joanie. It actually could work out much better for us."

"How do you mean?" I couldn't see anything positive in being left here on my own.

Verity pulled the dress over her head. Above the rustle of fabric I heard her say "Remember I said I was going to write to Gladys? The parlourmaid from the London house?"

"Yes." I was a little ashamed to realise I'd forgotten about that conversation we'd had.

"Well, I did. She may have received my letter by now."

"And?"

"Well, if Gladys is in London, I might be able to meet her there."

"Oh, I see." I pulled myself into a sitting position reluctantly. "Well, I suppose that would be a step forward." I paused, thinking. "What a shame I won't be able to join you."

"No, I suppose not." Verity had her nightdress on by now and was rolling down her stockings. "Although – I wonder if I could persuade Mrs

Anstells to let you have some time off, enough time to come down to London and stay overnight?"

I bit back the remark that I wanted to make, that it wasn't just the question of getting the time off but also of the train fare. Again, Verity did her mind-reading trick. "Don't worry about the fare, Joan. I've been saving up, and Dorothy's been quite generous lately."

I looked at her gratefully. "Well, I suppose it's worth a try."

"That's *if* we even go." Verity balled up the dirty stockings in her hand and stuffed them into the string bag in which she kept her dirty washing. "Anyway, that's not the only reason I want to go to London."

"What is the other?"

Verity sat back down on the bed and looked directly at me. "I want to go to Somerset House."

I felt a prickle of something – excitement? Anxiety? "Somerset House? Why?"

"I want to look up a will."

As soon as she said that, I knew why. I arched an eyebrow. "Let me guess. You want to look up the will of Lady Alice Cartwright."

Verity grinned. "You're so sharp you'll cut yourself, one day, Joanie."

I smiled back. "That's a good idea. Will they let you, though?"

"Oh yes," Verity said seriously. "Wills are a

matter of public record. Remember when I looked up Delphine Denford's?"

That name reminded me of something else. "He knows about us. The inspector, I mean."

"What do you mean he *knows* about us?"

"Inspector Marks. He mentioned it the other day, the fact he knew we were involved with the Asharton Manor case."

Now it was Verity's turn to raise an eyebrow. "Oh, yes? How peculiar that he mentioned it."

"I'm not sure if he thought it was admirable or just a big joke."

"Hmm." Verity gathered all the hairpins she'd taken from her hair and put them in the little glass pot on the dressing table. "Goodness knows it wasn't much of a joke at the time. I'm lucky I kept my position."

I made a noise of agreement. The scandal of the Asharton Manor case had been such that even as witnesses, Verity and I had been a little tainted by it. It had been a major worry of mine after the trial that I might not be able to find another job because of what had happened.

"It was exciting though, wasn't it?" I spoke a little wistfully. "Not the trial, I mean, but when we – when we were there, getting the evidence."

Verity smiled. "Yes, it certainly was." She giggled. "You know what, Joan, I think it's given us a taste for it."

I laughed too, thinking of that silly thing I'd told the inspector. "Well, everyone has to have a hobby."

That made us both snort and then we both looked nervously at the door, wondering whether we were making too much noise. For some reason, I thought of Nora.

"Have you decided what we can do to help Nora?"

Verity sobered up immediately. "We'll try all the usual stuff first. And then if that doesn't work—" She stopped talking for a moment. "I've got another idea."

"What?"

Verity shook her head. "I won't say just yet, Joan. You wouldn't like it."

"Oh." I was silent, on fire with curiosity. But somehow I managed not to pry. Then my train of thought went back to my imaginings in the kitchen this morning. "Has Nora told you who the father is?" I asked. For some reason, I almost whispered.

Verity shook her head. "No. She hasn't mentioned him."

"Do you know who it is?"

Verity raised one shoulder in a half shrug. "No... not really. I've got a few ideas."

I waited for her to tell me but she didn't. So I told her, very tentatively, what I'd thought that morning.

"Of course, I know it's my imagination running away with me," I said at the end. "But it just gave me a turn to even think it." I appealed to Verity rather desperately. "You don't think I'm right, do you, V?"

Verity had gone a little pale. "No, of course I don't, Joan. Nora would never do such a wicked thing, I'm sure." She looked thoughtful for a moment. "Although, you've just given me an idea."

"What's that?"

"Well, we – and the police, of course – have been working on the assumption that Peter Drew's murder is related to the murder of Lady Eveline."

"Well, it must be," I reasoned. Then I told Verity what I'd seen those few days ago, Peter Drew sneaking out of a bedroom that wasn't his. "He was a snooper. He must have found out something about the killer."

Verity had her head on one side. "That's logical, yes, but what if – what if the second murder is about something else entirely? That it's *not* related to the murder of Lady E at all?"

I stared at her. "Maybe," I said doubtfully.

She must have heard my scepticism. "Of course, it probably is," she added hastily.

Something else occurred to me. "Oh, V, the money. Remember the money?"

"What money?"

I couldn't believe I'd only just remembered this. "Dorothy said that Peter told her he was getting hold of some money, remember?"

Verity was frowning. "But that was because he thought he was inheriting, wasn't it?"

I shook my head. "That's what *we* thought. But what if it was because he was blackmailing someone, because he knew something about the killer?"

We were both staring across the room at one another, tense with excitement.

"Yes," said Verity, eventually. "That does make sense."

I jumped off the bed and started walking around the room, forgetting I was half-dressed. "Who has an alibi for the time of Peter Drew's murder?"

"Duncan Cartwright does. He was out at his club all evening. That's definite." Verity looked into space, clearly trying to recall something. "Dorothy – well, she was in bed. I was with her for some of the evening but not the whole of it. But she couldn't have done it, V. She just...she just isn't that sort of person."

"I know." I realised that I was half in and half out of my dress, tutted, and began to unbutton the rest of the fastenings. "I know she wouldn't do something like that. Not stab her own brother."

Verity winced. "So that just leaves Lord C and Rosalind."

My dress slithered to the ground and I picked it up and shook it out. "You said they alibied each other. Again."

"Yes. But look here, Joanie, Rosalind can't have

anything to do with it. I saw her that night Lady Eveline was murdered."

"I know." I hung my dress up on the peg on the wall and turned to face Verity. I think we both realised what we were thinking but the realisation was too big, too huge to voice out loud.

A silence hung in the room and then Verity said, with a change of tone, "Gosh, it's awfully late. We both need to get some sleep."

I hesitated for a second, unwilling to let things drop. Then fatigue hit me in a grey wave and I yawned. "Yes. Yes, I suppose you're right. Let's turn in."

We completed our final ablutions for the night and then climbed into our beds, saying good night quite formally. Verity turned off the lamp.

I was just dropping off when her voice came through the darkness. "Don't worry, Joanie. We'll talk more tomorrow. I have a feeling we're almost there."

"I agree," I whispered. I waited for her to say more but nothing came, and then I yawned again, turned over under the blankets, and went to sleep.

Chapter Eighteen

JUST AS VERITY HAD PREDICTED, Dorothy managed to persuade Inspector Marks that it would be perfectly fine to allow her to go to London. As soon as it was confirmed, Verity came running for me and immediately dragged me off to see Mrs Anstells, to ask whether I could have the time off to accompany them. Mrs Anstells had frowned and pursed her lips, and hummed and hawed, but as I hadn't had very much time off lately, things being as they were, and with Verity's usual powers of persuasiveness (she and Dorothy made a fine team), permission was eventually granted for me to travel down with Verity in a few days' time.

In due course, we found ourselves on the train, third class of course, while Dorothy was ensconced up in first. I had made up some sandwiches, boiled some eggs and made a flask of tea for the journey. As the scenery rolled past the windows, and London came nearer and nearer, I could barely contain my excitement. It was so long since I'd journeyed anywhere further than Merisham village; just the thought of being somewhere different was exhilarating, let alone going to the capital city, with all its lights and noise and excitement.

Verity waited until we were almost at St. Pancras Station before she told me her news. "I've heard from Gladys," she said, grinning away. "She'll be meeting us tonight, at the café on Piccadilly."

I gaped. "That's fantastic. But won't Dorothy need you?"

Verity shook her head. "No, I've got to get her dressed and ready for dinner, but then she said I could go out for a few hours before I have to get back. She's off out to a jazz club, so goodness knows when she'll be back."

I frowned. It seemed a little unfeeling of Dorothy to be out whooping it up this soon after her brother's death – not to mention her mother's. Verity caught the expression on my face. "I know, Joan, but believe me, I think she's doing it as an escape. She just wants to run away from it all."

I nodded, not quite believing it. But it wasn't my place to say so. "What did Gladys say in her letter? Wasn't she terribly curious? Or anxious?"

Verity said nothing but reached into her bag and handed me an opened envelope. Curious, I drew out the single sheet of paper inside, smoothed it out and read it. *Dear Verity* (it ran) *I was ever so surprised to get your letter. Me mam passed it on to me here at Brookland House. It would be lovely to meet up with you again, you was always a good friend to me back when I was at his lordship's house. I don't miss them days, I can tell you. But enough of me going on. If you want to give me a call when you know when you will be in London, we can meet for a cuppa and a chat. It's Primrose 4368. It's just me and the cook here so we can get telephone calls with no bother. Take care, Gladys.*

I looked up at Verity. "So, you telephoned her?"

"Yes." Verity looked mischievous. "Snuck out to the village on one of Dorothy's errands and used the box by the post office."

I was still surprised at how readily Gladys had agreed to meet with us – or with Verity; I wasn't sure if Gladys knew I'd be there too. When I said as much to Verity, she shrugged. "Just leave the talking to me," she said. "Please, Joan."

I didn't mind. As the train began to enter the outskirts of London and draw closer to St. Pancras, it all started to feel a little bit like a dream. Were we really going to ask a maid who neither of us had seen for years whether she'd witnessed a murder? Shaking my head, I began to gather up our things as the train, clanking and shunting so that we staggered about the carriage, finally reached its destination.

There was a driver waiting for us at the station. It was some time since I'd been to London, and the hustle and bustle and noise and smoke was at first a little overwhelming. I helped Verity carry the cases of Dorothy's that the porter couldn't manage. It seemed an awful lot of luggage for a couple of nights' stay, but I remembered Verity telling me that when Dorothy was in town, it wasn't beyond her to change her outfit five times a day. Verity herself kept hold of the jewellery case and carried it close to her body. I eyed it nervously as we manoeuvred our way through the crowds. I didn't like to think of what the contents inside would be worth.

Eventually we arrived at the townhouse, a tall double-fronted Georgian building with smartly-painted black railings running along the front at street level. Of course, in the car, I'd sat up front with the driver and hadn't had much of a chance to even set eyes on Dorothy. Now, as I watched her walk up the steps to the front entrance, where the interim housekeeper waited to greet her, I thought she looked years older, the golden glow of her hair dulled, her high cheekbones almost protruding through the skin of her face. Despite the fact that she was walking through the imposing front door and I was walking down the basement steps to the servants' entrance, I pitied Dorothy. I felt ashamed of my unkind thoughts about her 'whooping it up'. Perhaps all she wanted to do was run away from everything, lose herself in cocktails and jazz music and handsome youths to dance with. I could understand that.

I went into the kitchen and re-introduced myself to the small number of kitchen staff. The Cartwrights kept on a skeleton staff when the family were not in residence: just a housekeeper on retainer wages, a cook, two housemaids and a footman. They were pleasant enough people but as I was only staying for the one night, I didn't want to waste time in small talk or, worst of all, get roped into helping out with the work of the house. No, this was my time off, and I intended to use it well. After a cup of tea, I carried my bags up to the room I'd be sharing with Edna, one of the two housemaids. I looked at the put-up cot that had been set up in the small space that wasn't taken up with Edna's bed and sighed. Oh well, it was only for one night. It made me almost nostalgic for our bare little room back at Merisham Lodge.

Verity and I set off to meet Gladys a few hours later. We had both changed out of our uniforms and as we set off down the road, I felt my spirits lift. A whole luxurious evening in which to eat a meal and drink tea and pretend I was something other than a servant for once. I was so light-hearted I'd almost forgotten why we were there in the first place.

The tea rooms were just off Piccadilly Circus, which was absolute bedlam. Motor cars rushed along the streets at a speed quite frightening to witness, and the crowds were so thick I was in constant fear of falling off the pavement into the oncoming traffic. At last we pushed and shoved our way through to the quieter street on which the café was situated.

"Goodness," Verity gasped, straightening her hat which had been knocked askew in the melee. "I hope Gladys turns up, after all this."

But we needn't have worried. Gladys was already sitting there at a table at the back, looking much as I remembered her. She had always had a slightly fast look about her, which was probably uncharitable of me, but remembering what Verity had told me about her, and what she used to get up to, perhaps not. Inevitably, my thoughts flew to Nora.

Gladys looked glad to see Verity and surprised to see me, although she greeted me quite pleasantly. The first few minutes were dashed away in trying to attract the attention of a nippy so we could place our order, always a bit of an undertaking in these busy places.

Finally, when we had sufficient tea and sandwiches and cake, Verity leaned forward over the table. "I know you were surprised to get my letter, eh, Gladys?"

"I should say so. I know you wrote me a beautiful card last Christmas but I'm ashamed to say I never wrote back. Sorry, Verity."

Verity waved a hand in the air. "Doesn't matter in the slightest." I was interested to note that her accent was changing very slightly as she spoke to Gladys. Verity spoke well, had always spoken well – that was her background and her education when growing up – but now her vowels were flattening slightly, she was almost dropping her 't's. I listened, fascinated, realising she was doing it to put Gladys at her ease.

"Now, Gladdie, you was always clever, I thought. Remember how we used to talk?" Gladys was nodding, chewing a scone at the same time. "Well," said Verity. "The thing is, we need your help. Me and Joanie, here."

Gladys chewed away, still nodding and looking inquisitive. So far, so good.

Verity went on. "You've heard about the murders, up at Merisham Lodge?"

"Not half!" said Gladys, through a shower of crumbs. "Gawd, it must have been awful. I can't see how you both have stuck it up there."

"It's been awful," Verity said with emphasis and shot me a significant look.

"Awful!" I intoned, dutifully.

Gladys' eyes had that peculiar gleam of someone wanting to know all the gory details without quite being brave enough to admit it. "Was it true that Lady Cartwright had her head clean bashed in?"

"Cor, yes, it certainly was." Verity was leaning

forward on her elbows, her eyes fixed on Gladys's prurient face. "Awful, it was. Let me tell you all about it."

It was while Verity was laying the groundwork for what she was going to ask Gladys, telling her all about the murders and the police and what Mr Fenwick had said and how we were all going in fear of our lives, I suddenly realised Gladys had no idea why we were really here. She didn't know what Verity and I were going to ask her. I had another blinding flash of insight then. Perhaps if Gladys had been told beforehand, she wouldn't have come.

Verity's tale wound to a close. Gladys' eyes were as round as the plate she was eating from. "So, the police have got no idea who done it?" she asked, her mouth hanging open.

Verity shook her head, her eyebrows raised in a kind of 'did you *ever*?' way. I bit back a giggle.

Gladys' gaze fell on the remaining scone. I pushed it towards her, silently.

"Thing is," Verity said, deceptively casually. "The inspector – ever such a handsome man, he is – he thinks it might all be to do with what happened to Lady Alice. You know. When she died." She sank her voice to a thrilling whisper. "You know, he thinks that might not have been an *accident*."

She sat back again, with her arms folded under her bosom, just like a gossiping washerwoman. I wanted to laugh again but one look at Gladys' face stopped me. She'd gone to pick up the scone and then dropped it.

"The police think that?" Gladys asked in a small voice.

Verity nodded. "They just can't *prove* it. They don't have a witness, you see. It's such a shame. There's us up there with some *lunatic* on the loose and who knows who's going to be next. Eh, Joan?" She looked across at me and I hastily agreed.

There was a short silence at our table, noticeable only to us in the tumult and hubbub of the busy café. I began to think that Verity might have overshot the mark, been too obvious, scared Gladys off. I think she thought so too because she leant forward even further.

"Gladdie. Gladdie, we have to know. Did you see something that night Lady Alice died? We have to know, Glad, you have to tell us. Our *lives* are in danger here."

Gladys looked as though she were about to cry. I opened my mouth but Verity beat me to it. When she next spoke, the working class accent had gone. Instead, she spoke in the precise, steely tones of someone born to the aristocracy. She could have been Dorothy herself. "Gladys Smith. If you know something, you have to tell us. *Tell us*."

Gladys' mouth was pinched and trembling. Verity's tone changed, just as suddenly. She still spoke in those same upper-class accents but her voice softened and became warm and calm. She put a hand on Gladys' trembling hand. "Gladdie, if you know something, you'd best not keep it to yourself. You could get into terrible trouble with the police, if they thought you were holding something back. Not to mention, well, it might actually put you in *danger*." I was impressed at how wide and aghast Verity could make her eyes. She really should have been on the stage. "Tell us, Gladdie, and we can help you."

Gladys dropped her eyes to her plate and the uneaten scone. She whispered something so quietly I couldn't hear what she said.

"What's that?" Verity asked, still in that tender tone.

Gladys looked up. Her rather small eyes were brimming with tears. "I saw him," she whispered. "I saw him on the stairs. He was loosening the top rod, you know, the carpet rod, on the top stair."

Her voice died away. I held my breath. Verity leaned forward so that she was almost breathing in Gladys' ear and whispered "Saw who?"

Gladys looked terrified. For a moment, I thought she was going to refuse to answer but then I guessed that now she'd come to the pass, there was a relief in telling her secret. "Lord Cartwright."

I clenched my fist in triumph under the table. *I knew it*. With difficulty I restrained myself from thumping the table and shouting 'yes!'

Verity behaved impeccably. She drew back a little and said, with just the right amount of shock in her voice, "Lord C? Are you sure?"

Gladys nodded jerkily. She started to speak, at first hesitantly and then faster and faster, the words almost spilling out. I got the impression she'd been bottling this up for years, unable to tell anyone her awful secret. Now that the stopper was out of the bottle, all the rest of it was gushing out.

We sat there for another couple of hours, buying more tea and cakes, getting the whole story out of poor, silly Gladys. How she'd been out the evening Lady Alice died, how she'd gone for a walk with Fred, who used to deliver the vegetables – *you remember him, Verity, don't you?* – and how she'd got back late, so late that if Mrs Anstells had caught her coming in she would have been dismissed and no mistake. The kitchen door had already been locked for the night. How Gladys had had to come in the front door, lifting the latch, creeping through the darkened hallway like a mouse, trying to get to the servants' stairs before being caught. And she'd looked up at a dark shape on the stairs, right at the top, bending over the stairs with a lamp in his hand, doing something to the stair rod on the top stair.

"You're sure it was Lord C?" Verity asked.

Gladys nodded. "It was him. I could see his face plain as day in the lamplight."

That night, Lady Alice had fallen down the

stairs and broken her neck. Gladys had given her notice the next day. I didn't have to ask her why or ask her why she hadn't said anything to anyone. Who would have believed the tweeny – the lowest ranking of the servants – over Lord Arthur Saint-John Cartwright? Let alone how Gladys would have had to explain *why* she was coming in so late. That alone would have been enough for her dismissal without a reference.

Of course, after all the story came out, we had to spend another hour calming Gladys down and reassuring her that she wouldn't get into trouble for telling us. Verity spoke very heartily of what a good man the inspector was and how Gladys would be in his good books if she just told him what she'd told us and how everyone would be so pleased and so grateful to her for helping catch a ruthless killer. Why, Gladys would practically be the heroine of the day! It wouldn't surprise Verity to hear that she might even get a medal or a commendation for being so brave.

I thought this was laying it on a bit thick but I could see that Gladys was drinking it in. I felt a qualm of conscience that Verity didn't mention anything about having to give evidence, or having to go to court, or anything like that. But perhaps she was right to do that. This was serious, after all, and if Gladys was scared off, nothing would happen.

Eventually we parted, having assured Gladys

that we would be in touch and would put a good word in for her with the inspector and that no, she wouldn't get into trouble for telling him, or us, or indeed anyone, and in fact, it was the safest and wisest thing to do. Verity went so far as to escort Gladys back to the house where she worked and saw her safely inside. Then she turned and came back up the steps to where I was waiting in the street.

She said nothing to me but took my arm.

"Well," I began, but Verity shook her head.

"Let's talk later," she said. "It's probably not a good idea to discuss this out in public."

"Oh, yes." I felt silly that this hadn't occurred to me. I took her silence as a cue and we walked back to the Cartwright townhouse in utter quiet, our minds awhirl.

Chapter Nineteen

OF COURSE, I SHOULD HAVE known we wouldn't have had a chance to discuss it further that night. Verity had to wait up for Dorothy, in Dorothy's room, and I just couldn't see how I could make my way up there without rousing the curiosity and, more importantly, the disapproval of Mrs Cookson, the housekeeper. Of course, Verity and I weren't sharing a room, so we didn't even have a chance to talk when she finally came to bed. Goodness knows what time that actually was. All I knew was that Verity didn't appear at breakfast, and after breakfast it was time for me to catch the train back to Merisham again.

I took the bus to King's Cross with a heavy heart. I'd so much wanted to discuss what Gladys had told us with Verity, and now she wouldn't be back to Merisham for another three days. I checked I had my return ticket, adjusted my gloves and picked up my overnight bag, a cast-off of Dorothy's that Verity has passed onto me. The return journey wasn't nearly as much fun as the ride down. For one thing, I was alone – as alone as you can be in a crowded third class carriage – and for another, I was heading back to go straight back into work. At least, I consoled myself, there would only be Lord Cartwright, Duncan and Rosalind to cook for. I couldn't imagine they would be up to entertaining, not under the circumstances.

As the train steamed its way northwards, I folded my gloved hands in my lap and tried to think. What to do now? Surely the first thing was to go and see Inspector Marks and tell him what Gladys had told us? Again, I wished fervently that Verity and I could have discussed it before parting. I knew that she was planning to go to Somerset House to look up the will of Lady Alice Cartwright. Was it possible, I wondered, for me to be able to telephone her? I didn't think I could bear to wait three days before we could speak again, not at such a crucial point in the proceedings.

Accordingly, when I stepped off the train at Merisham, I walked briskly to the nearest telephone box. Anxiously, I counted up my money and was thankful to find I had just enough for a call. I put in the coppers, waited for the operator and gave the number of the Cartwrights' London house. Then I waited, telephone receiver slipping in my damp hands, praying that Verity was at home and able to come to the telephone.

The footman, James, answered and I asked to speak to Lady Dorothy's maid. Without giving my name, I tried to sound like another lady's maid, as if I was telephoning about something quite respectable, arranging a visit to the London Hydro, for example, or a fashion parade.

James was no Mr Fenwick. He went off obediently to fetch Verity and, miracle of miracles, a few minutes later I heard her familiar voice on the end of the phone.

"V, it's me, Joan. I can't talk for long, the pips will go any moment."

"Oh *hello*, there, Constance. How nice to hear from you. Her ladyship *will* be pleased."

For a moment I thought she'd taken leave of her senses and then realised she was saying that for the benefit of anyone who might be listening at her end.

"V, I'm going to go and see Inspector Marks. I'll tell him what Gladys told us. Is that right? Should I do that?"

"That would be delightful," said Verity's voice. "Yes, I do think that's a jolly good idea. I'll be sure to let her ladyship know."

The pips began to sound in my ear. "Don't forget about Somerset House," was all I managed to hiss before we were cut off.

I replaced the dead receiver with a mingled sense of relief and annoyance. At least I knew that Verity approved of my next course of action. As I pushed open the heavy door of the telephone booth, it occurred to me to wonder just how pleased Inspector Marks would be at our amateurish attempts at investigation. Would he be cross that we'd been forward enough to even think of approaching a witness? Or, perhaps worse, would he laugh?

I could see the blue lamp of the police station across the road but at that moment, I remained on the other side, suddenly feeling as if going there was a very bad idea. What if Verity and I were wrong? What if Gladys was lying? What if she *were* telling the truth but that despite our urgings, she refused to talk to the police or even see them? Was I really and truly getting ideas above my station? What did I think Verity and I could do that the police couldn't?

I think I might have stayed there all afternoon, oblivious to the time ticking away, if not for a sharp shower of rain that came along. The cold spatter of drops against my face and hat made me grit my teeth and finally make up my mind. I checked that the road was clear and ran across the rutted surface to the police station entrance.

Entering the building, I was reminded of the time Verity and I had gone to a similar sized station during the events at Asharton Manor. As I crossed the threshold, I could feel my earlier jitters vanish. When Verity and I had first entered a police station we'd both been nervous, expecting to see hardened criminals being wrestled to the floor. Of course, it hadn't been anything like that. Just as then, the station here today was quiet, just one person by the front desk, apparently reporting a missing dog.

I waited until the desk was clear and then stepped up, beginning to feel nervous again. I asked for Inspector Marks.

To my surprise, he was actually at the station and available to see me. He strode into the reception area and greeted me pleasantly, although I could just ascertain a slight flicker of apprehension visible behind his professional smile.

"Miss Hart. What can I do for you?"

I asked if we could speak privately. He ushered me through to a bare little room beyond the reception area, furnished only with a table and two chairs. There was a good fire in the grate though, and I loosened the neck of my coat.

"Miss Hart?"

Now I had come to the sticking point, I felt myself wanting to prevaricate, even to say that it was nothing – nothing important. But I knew that wasn't the case.

"Inspector, Verity – Miss Hunter – and I have recently been to London. I've just returned from there. While we were there, we met with someone who I believe could be an important witness."

The inspector's face remained steady but his neatly trimmed beard quivered. "Indeed, Miss Hart?"

I faced him fully then, folding my hands on the table in front of me. Slowly and carefully, I told him exactly what we had done: surmised a motive in the death of Lady Alice Cartwright, which recalled to Verity the fact that there may have been a witness to the crime and the fact that we had managed to make contact with this witness and, indeed, managed to persuade her that it was her duty to talk to the police.

As I spoke, I could see the inspector's dark eyes watching me keenly. It was a new experience for me, to have someone of influence hanging on my every word. I was almost alarmed to find how much I enjoyed it.

When I finished speaking, the inspector sat silently for a moment. Then he leant forward. "What is this girl's full name?" he rapped out.

Silently, I passed him the card upon which Verity had written down Gladys' particulars. He took it, scanned it quickly, and put it aside. For a moment, he seemed to be struggling to find the right words.

"That's all I had to say, sir," I said, when the silence stretched out for an uncomfortably long time.

The inspector rasped a hand through his beard, staring at me. "May I hear this theory of yours, Miss Hart?"

I swallowed. "As to who I believe the murderer is, sir?"

"Correct."

I refolded my hands, which had suddenly started trembling. Then I told him.

"I see." He stared at me in a way I couldn't interpret. Then, in a move that made me jump, he sprang to his feet. "Thank you, Miss Hart. You can be sure we'll follow up the information you've given us."

I was clearly being dismissed. Scarlet-cheeked, I felt very foolish. I got up, fumbling for my bag. I hadn't even taken off my gloves.

He ushered me to the door and opened it for me. I felt a horrid tumult of emotions: guilt, shame, anxiety, a keen sense of my own ridiculousness. Who did I think I was, making such accusations? I almost stumbled in my haste to leave the room.

I was almost at the door of the station, holding back tears, when I heard the inspector call my name. I gulped and turned.

Quickly he crossed the tiled floor of the station until he was close to me. Then he leant forward and gently took hold of my elbow. I felt my face grow hot again.

"Miss Hart," he said, in a completely different tone to the one he'd just used to say goodbye. "May I just say one thing?"

I looked up at him, uncomprehending. Inspector Marks squeezed my arm.

"Please be careful," he said. "Please, for the love

of God, don't tell anyone what you've just told me. Promise me."

"I – I will—" I stuttered.

"*Please*. I don't want the next body we find to be yours."

I stared at him, wide-eyed. Then, because at that moment I was incapable of speech, I nodded and disengaged myself before letting myself out of the door of the police station.

Chapter Twenty

IT SEEMED AN AGE UNTIL Verity and Dorothy returned from London, although it was really only two days later. It was late afternoon when they arrived, and I was busy in the kitchen. Maggie and I were preparing the tray for tea. As I arranged the cups and saucers I felt a pang that there were now only four, rather than the six that had been there all those weeks ago, the last time I'd carried it up, when Lady Eveline had still been alive, and Peter Drew too.

Albert came in to the kitchen and I handed him the tray. As he bore it from the room with some ceremony, I heaved a sigh.

"So sad, Joanie?"

The voice behind me made me shriek. I turned and there was Verity, smiling and rosy-cheeked from the cold air outside.

"You're back!"

We hugged. She wore a smart new blue velvet

cloche and a nice sparkly brooch pinned to the lapel of her dark blue coat.

"Coo, nice," I said, gesturing to it. Verity looked down and half-smiled.

"Dorothy's gift. She didn't want it anymore."

For a moment, I felt envious of her job. Imagine having the kind of position where you routinely got lovely jewellery and hats and clothes from your mistress, just because she didn't want them anymore.

"Listen," Verity said hurriedly. "I only came down to get a pot of tea and some biscuits, I've got to go straight back up. I think I'll be down for dinner though, so let's talk then."

"Very well." I had my own work to get to. I gave her arm a friendly squeeze and was just about to walk back to the table when she leant in and murmured something.

"What's that?"

"Did you talk to you-know-who?"

Discreet Verity. I remembered Inspector Mark's admonition and nodded. "I'll tell you later."

She gave me a nod and a wink and went to find a teapot.

I flew through the rest of my chores with a feverish impatience, just wanting to get to dinner so that Verity and I could talk. As luck would have it, because Dorothy was back, Rosalind suddenly decreed that we needed a much fancier dinner than the one we'd had planned. I cursed her freely inside my head as Mrs Watling and Maggie and I ran hither and thither from the stove to the refrigerator, from the pantry to the larder. I even had to replenish our vegetable stocks from the root cellar. Maggie flatly refused to go down there by herself so I ended up doing the trip instead, just to save time.

I paused on the top step, looking down into the darkness beneath me. Then I flicked on the light. Its meagre glow did nothing to dispel the qualm of fear I felt about descending into the cellar depths. Of course, I knew there was no corpse here now, nothing nastier than a spider or two lying in wait for me around the corner of the passageway. Even so... I could feel my steps faltering as I walked down the dusty brick staircase.

I was pretty sure that there would be no more murders. Pretty sure – but not certain. What if I were wrong? I thought I knew the motive for both murders, but perhaps I was wrong? I wasn't a detective, after all.

I took a deep breath and hurried down to the cellar floor, scurrying along the corridor to grab the sack of onions and potatoes that we needed. I kept my eyes fixed firmly on the bags of vegetables in my hand. Try as I might, I couldn't help but recall being here before, when we'd seen Peter Drew's dead body. Shaking, I wheeled around and ran back to the steps and up to safety and warmth and light.

The servants' dinner that night was mostly refashioned leftovers from lunch – Mrs Watling and I had no time to do anything more elaborate after the fancy dinner we'd had to prepare. Nobody complained though, just got stuck into eating. Verity was sitting in her usual place and caught my eye as I sat down. I flashed her a quick smile as I began to eat, thinking that we'd have to wait until bedtime to actually talk. There was no privacy in this place, none at all.

It was after dinner that I saw Verity with Nora in the corridor outside the kitchen. I could see something had changed hands, from Verity to Nora, a small white cardboard box. Nora slipped it into her apron pocket. They talked for a moment, both looking serious and then Nora hurried away.

"What was that all about?"" I murmured as Verity caught up with me.

She shook her head minutely. "Something I got her from London. Hopefully it'll help."

Guiltily, I realised I'd almost forgotten about poor Nora's predicament in the excitement of everything else that had happened. I was about to say something about wanting to help when the bell for Dorothy's room jangled loudly above our heads, and Verity cursed and set off for the stairs at a run.

At the end of a long, weary day, I climbed the stairs to the top floor, feeling the ache in my feet and in the small of my back as if tiny, cruel hands were wringing out the muscles there. Wearily, I limped along the corridor to our room, wondering whether I even had the energy to wash. Verity was already there, unpacking her London bag.

"Goodness, Joan, you look all in. Here—" She put her hand into the inner pocket of her case and drew something out, handing it to me. I looked down at the bar of chocolate.

"Oh, thank you," I said, truly grateful. I slit the paper, broke off a piece for Verity and then sat down on my bed to enjoy my treat. The sweet taste seemed to re-energise me, lighting me up like a candle.

"That's better," I said after a few minutes. Verity smiled.

"Thought that would do you good." She finished putting her clothes away, lining up her shoes neatly on the floor of the wardrobe. "By the way..." She shot me a look that warned me that what she had to say was serious. I sat up a little.

"What is it?"

"I know who the father is."

"Of Nora's baby?" I swallowed. "Who?"

Verity sighed. "It's Benton."

"*Benton*? Duncan Cartwright's *valet*?" I was

flabbergasted. He'd never seemed to take more than a minute's notice of Nora that I had ever seen.

"Told you he was a goat." Verity sat down heavily on her bed, looking suddenly exhausted. "Of course, he's wanting nothing more to do with her, the b— " She caught my eye and looked away. "Sorry, Joan. But honestly. Nora really thought he was in love with her. Such a *fool*." She said it fiercely, and I wasn't sure if she were referring to Nora or to Benton.

I brushed a crumb of chocolate from my chin. "What was it that you got her from London?"

Verity sighed again. "Pennyroyal pills. They might work... Then again, they might not."

"Oh." I was quiet for a moment, thinking. If the pills didn't work, then what on Earth was Nora going to do?

Eventually Verity heaved herself upright and began to undress. "So, you went to Inspector Marks, then?" she asked quietly.

I nodded and told her what had happened, conscientiously including both his dismissive goodbye and then his oddly fervent final words to me.

"Hmm," said Verity, chewing her lip. "I wonder..."

"What do you mean?"

"Nothing. I just – I wonder what's going to happen."

"Yes." I pulled off my cuffs and began to unpin my cap. "I know what you mean. How did you get on at Somerset House, by the way?"

Verity pulled her nightdress on over her head. "Just as we thought, Joanie. Lord Cartwright was the main beneficiary of Lady Alice's will."

"Hmm." I wondered whether the police knew that. But of course they would. Wouldn't they?

We finished our ablutions and then got into our beds. I was feeling...strange. Sort of restless. Anxious. But I couldn't put my finger on why.

We said good night and turned off the lamp. Verity's breathing soon deepened into sleep but I lay there in the dark, despite my weariness, for what seemed like hours. There was something nagging at me, like a tiny pain somewhere in my body that I couldn't quite locate. A minor itch that I couldn't scratch. Again and again, I tried to pinpoint what it was that was bothering me, but I couldn't quite find it. Eventually, I think I fell asleep through sheer frustration.

Chapter Twenty One

THINGS BEGAN HAPPENING VERY RAPIDLY the next day. It was early afternoon, with the chaos of luncheon just behind us, when the police arrived. Mrs Watling and I were just taking the last of the dishes into the scullery for Maggie to wash up when we heard the clatter of the bells on the police cars outside.

We stopped what we were doing and stared at each other. I put down the pot I was holding onto the table and pelted for the door, without asking Mrs Watling if I could leave. I *had* to know what was happening.

I ran into Verity in the upstairs corridor. Her eyes wide, she pulled me back behind the shadow of the staircase as the urgent peal of the doorbell sounded. We held our breath, out of sight but not out of hearing, as Mr Fenwick opened the door.

Inspector Marks's voice said, sternly, "I must see his lordship, Fenwick. Is he in?"

"He's in the drawing room, Inspector." I could

hear the surprise and the disquiet in Mr Fenwick's voice. There was the sound of many footsteps, almost marching, down the corridor and out of earshot.

Verity was still clutching my arms. We looked at each other and then, as one, moved into the hallway and tiptoed down the corridor towards the drawing room. The door was ajar – they had only just gone in.

I held my breath, trying to listen over the thunder of blood in my ears.

"Lord Cartwright, I must ask you to accompany me to the station to answer some questions," Inspector Marks said.

I heard a female gasp but couldn't tell if it came from Dorothy or Rosalind. There was a splutter from Lord Cartwright. "I will do no such thing, Inspector. How dare you march into my house and—"

Inspector Marks cut across him and his voice had steel in it. "Then I'm afraid you leave me no choice. Lord Cartwright, I'm arresting you for the murder of Lady Alice Cartwright. You do not have to say anything, but anything you say may be used at your trial. You'll be given full facilities to communicate with your solicitor."

There was a shocked cry – definitely Rosalind this time. I could see the soundless gape on my face echoed on Verity's. Shaking off her hand, I moved closer, close enough to look through the gap in the doorway. I could only see the back of Inspector Marks's suit but beyond him I could see Duncan Cartwright. He was white to the lips.

I had expected a roar from Lord Cartwright. I had expected *something*. But there was no sound at all, a silence that was as chilling as it was unexpected. Verity crept up to stand beside me and we both listened with all our might.

There was the shift of feet and I saw Inspector Marks move forward. The door began to open wider and Verity and I turned tail and ran for our lives towards the kitchen – or at least ran for our positions. We flew past the front door and clattered down the stairs to the basement, so shocked we were barely breathing.

YOU CAN IMAGINE WHAT IT was like in the servants' hall that afternoon. Everyone talked at once, or shouted, rather, until finally Mr Fenwick and Mrs Anstells managed to restore a little order. Nancy had an attack of the vapours and had to be brought round with a cold flannel and Mrs Anstell's smelling salts. Even after everyone had somewhat calmed down, the whispers and insinuations went around and around, coiling through the rooms below like smoke carried on a breeze. *Well, I never liked him; always had a temper; Lady Alice was so sweet; it must have been him; it's like the Brides in the Bath, once a man gets a taste for it he doesn't stop...*

Mr Fenwick said threateningly that anyone caught discussing *anything* to do with his lordship would be dismissed without a reference. We all subsided, muttering darkly. I caught Verity's eyes across the room and we exchanged a wordless glance of mingled pride and anxiety. We had done this, hadn't we? The police had to have arrested him because of the new evidence obtained from Gladys' testimony, surely? And if Lord Cartwright had killed his first wife, then surely that pointed to him having killed his second?

Of course, everyone went on discussing it. We were just careful to do it out of earshot of Mr Fenwick. Verity cornered me by the door to the root cellar and dragged me into the storeroom next to it.

She shut the door and leant on it. "Joan, this is it. I can't believe it. I know we were both thinking it..."

She trailed off and we stared at one another. Of course she was right. I had been thinking it, that Lord Cartwright had to have been the murderer, but it had just seemed too big and too frightening a truth to say.

I took in a deep breath. "He got rid of his first wife, all right. Why do you think he did it?"

"Easy," said Verity cynically. "He wanted to marry Lady Eveline but Lady Alice wouldn't give him a divorce. Or maybe *he* didn't want the scandal of a divorce and he wanted to inherit his wife's money."

"Yes." I began pacing up and down the small area of the storeroom, twisting my hands. "So why murder Lady Eveline?"

"Why do you think? Because he wants to marry Rosalind, of course. And just like before, he gets to inherit his present wife's fortune."

"Yes." I came to a standstill and looked at Verity. That all made perfect sense. But then, why did I still have this small knot of uneasiness inside me?

Verity sensed that something was wrong. "Joan, the police wouldn't go and arrest a lord without really compelling evidence. They just *wouldn't*. So they have to know he's guilty."

"I know," I said, helplessly.

"So, what's wrong?"

"I don't know. I just feel—" I stopped. I didn't know how I felt. "What about Peter? Why kill him too?"

Verity rolled her eyes. Perhaps I really was being very stupid. "Blackmail, of course. Peter knew something, was blackmailing his stepfather, so he had to die."

"Yes." I found I was staring ahead of me without really seeing anything.

"Joan. It'll be all right. We've done the right thing."

"I know—"

There was a sharp knock on the door which made us both jump. Then Mrs Anstells' voice said "What are you girls doing in there? Come out at once."

We both grabbed something from the shelves – I took a stack of tea-towels and Verity picked up a box of candles. Then we opened the door.

"Sorry Mrs Anstells," Verity said cheerfully. "Joan and I were just getting some supplies."

Mrs Anstells gave us a sharp look but we both looked the picture of innocence. She stepped back to allow us past her. "Go about your work, then."

We both walked quickly, but hopefully not guiltily, down the corridor towards the kitchen. I didn't dare say anything else to Verity. She gave me an expressive look before she turned to take the stairs that led upstairs.

"We'll do a plain supper tonight for the family," Mrs Watling said. She sounded very flat, as if all her energy had gone. "I'm not up to doing much at all, God help me. What a day."

"I know." I tried to sound soothing.

"We'll all have to have a cold supper. You can get on with that now."

I nodded. At least that wouldn't be very strenuous. It was just as well; I felt stretched, strange – as if sparks might come shooting out of my fingers. When I lifted up a saucepan I was surprised my fingers didn't leave dents in the metal.

As I prepared the servants' supper, I could still

feel that tight knot of anxiety deep within me. Why? Lord Cartwright had been arrested. He was safely away from us, in police custody. There would be no more murders. So why was I feeling so uneasy?

As we all sat down to our cold supper that night, I was feeling no better. I didn't know whether Verity would make it down that night – with things being as they were, perhaps Dorothy would prefer to keep her upstairs with her – but she appeared in the doorway just as we were all gathering around the table.

"We will not be discussing anything at this table tonight," said Mr Fenwick sternly as we all sat down. "I don't believe that any topic of conversation would be suitable at this moment in time. Please be so good as to eat your meal in silence."

Nobody argued with him. We all sat and chewed our food, our minds busy with our own thoughts. I cut a slice of ham and lifted it onto my plate. As I ate, I let my eyes wander around the table, looking at everyone's faces. Nancy was red-eyed and sniffled occasionally. Albert looked worried. I let my gaze drift around further to where Nora was sat, next to Benton.

It was the first time I'd seen them together since Verity's revelation of their relationship. Curious, I watched them, wondering whether I'd be able to guess that they'd once been romantically involved, if I didn't already know. No, I decided, there was no possible way I'd ever be able to ascertain their involvement. They were sitting in a way that reminded me of something, both their bodies turned slightly away from one another, as if they had to hold that side of themselves stiff. As if they disliked one another.

I put the fork in my hand down on my plate with a musical chime on the china. Watching Nora and Benton ostentatiously ignore one another was giving me a cold feeling. That knot of anxiety that I'd had within me was growing, beginning to flower. I could feel an iciness creeping up my legs, as if I were sitting in a draft. It crept up and flowed into the pit of my stomach, flooding it as if I'd swallowed a pint of icy water. Why? What was it about the two of them that made me so uneasy?

Then I remembered who it was they reminded me of. The knowledge actually made me flinch, so much so that my chair jerked back from the table with a wooden shriek. I leapt to my feet and everybody looked at me in surprise.

I spoke so shakily that it gave credence to my words. "I'm sorry, Mr Fenwick but I'm not feeling well. May I be excused?"

He raised his bushy eyebrows but nodded. I shot Verity a glance as I hurried away, and as I left the room, I could hear her asking Mr Fenwick if she could be excused too, to see if I was all right.

I hurried along the corridor to the privy and

went inside. After just a moment, I heard Verity's voice outside.

"Joan? Are you all right?"

I opened the door. She eyed my face with increasing worry.

"What's the matter?"

"Can you get Nora? I urgently need to speak to her."

Verity's own mobile eyebrows shot up. She opened her mouth, probably to ask why, but I must have looked desperate because she shut it again and turned on her heel.

I shut the privy door while I waited. My heart was hammering. Was I right? I'd been so sure before but if I were wrong... I could hear two sets of footsteps coming back down the corridor and cracked open the door an inch.

"Thank you Nora, I could use your help," Verity was saying loudly, obviously for the benefit of Mrs Anstells. I wondered briefly if we were overdoing it. If she got too worried about me and my mysterious illness, Mrs Anstells would come along here herself and then everything would be ruined.

I opened up the door and pulled both Verity and Nora inside. Nora squeaked.

"Shut up!" I hissed. I took a moment to listen out for other footsteps. Nothing as yet.

I took a deep breath. "Nora, this is really

important. You remember the night that Lady Eveline died?"

Nora's dark eyes were wide. "What—"

"Just tell me!" I knew I sounded fierce but I couldn't help it. "Was Benton with you on the night Lady Eveline died?"

Nora went white, then scarlet. She looked at Verity, who had the grace to look a little ashamed.

"It doesn't matter about that," I said quickly, trying to make her understand. "I'm not judging you, I don't care. I just need to know if Benton was with you that night."

Nora blinked rapidly. "I don't—" she began.

I seized both her arms, not quite shaking her but the threat was there. Verity made a movement forward, as if to stop me, but I shot her a glare and she backed away, as far as she could in the confined space.

I spoke slowly and clearly. "Nora. Was Benton with you on the night Lady Eveline died?"

"I—" Nora hesitated. Then, tears brimming on the edge of her eyelids, she nodded.

I exhaled. "From what time?"

She spoke in a whisper. "I can't remember exactly."

"Try. You have to try."

"Well, I think it was about eleven o'clock, because we heard the clock in the hallway chime. You know, the one on the passageway below." She dropped her gaze. "We were in one of the guest rooms."

I still had hold of her arms. "Nora, how long did he...did Benton stay with you?"

Nora dropped her head again. Her cheeks were so red I could almost feel the heat coming off them. "For a couple of hours," she mumbled.

I let go of her arms, feeling weak. Now I knew.

Verity had stood there silently all this time. She was still silent but tense, coiled like a spring. I looked over at her.

"That's it, V." I opened my mouth to say more but realised Nora was still there. "Could you take Nora back to the table, do you think? I think I might be going to be sick."

Nora hurried out of her own accord. Verity paused in the doorway. "What the hell's going on, Joan?"

I put a hand up to my forehead. My fingers were shaking. "Firstly, can you try and stop Nora telling anyone what I just asked her?"

"I'll try. But—"

I cut across her. "I need to talk to the inspector. Right now."

"Now?" Verity shook her head. "How on Earth are you going to do that?"

"I don't know." I felt like hitting the privy wall in frustration. "I can't telephone, I don't even know if he's at the police station..."

Verity was chewing her lip. We stared at one another in silence for a minute, my hands clenched, until Verity suddenly gave a yelp. "Oh! I know where he is. Dorothy told me he's staying at The Brown Cow." It was one of the inns in the village. I felt a leap of gladness but that was almost immediately quashed.

"How am I going to get there? I can't just leave."

Verity suddenly looked resolute. "I'm taking you to the doctor," she said, firmly. "You're ill and you need to see him."

I drew in a shaky breath. "Do you think that will work?"

Verity blew out her cheeks with a puff of air. "Joan, I'm not clairvoyant. It might work, it might mean we get dismissed. But it sounds as though it's important." She grinned suddenly and said, "And I want to know everything anyway, and this is the only way we're going to be able to talk."

I looked at her for a moment and then half-laughed. It was almost a sob. "You're right that it's important. It could be a matter of life or death."

"Well," said Verity. "Let's go, then. Look as ill as you can."

We stumbled out of the privy with Verity's arm supporting me. I clutched my stomach and groaned. As we passed the sideboard which stood by the kitchen door, Verity pulled me to a stop. "Wait," she whispered and then dunked her hand into a half-full glass of water that stood with the other dirty dishes on top of the sideboard. Then she swiped her wet hand over my brow. "Let's go," she whispered and we stumbled on, back into the kitchen, me groaning away like an old, sick sheep.

"I CAN'T *BELIEVE* THAT WORKED," VERITY said breathlessly as we sped away through the darkness, only the bobbing light of a hand-held oil lamp to guide our way.

"I know. Perhaps I'm a better actress than I thought."

Verity giggled. "You know they all probably think you're pregnant. Or having terrible trouble with your bowels."

That made me laugh. "I know."

We had reached the stile by now. The night was huge all around us, the wind shaking the trees like a giant invisible hand ruffling the woods. Verity climbed over and offered me her hand.

"Thank you." I jumped down, feeling the shock in my ankles as my feet hit the ground. I felt as if I'd been filled with champagne – I was fizzing with energy.

"So, what *is* going on?" Verity tucked my arm underneath hers and pulled me forward.

I told her. She was so shocked she stopped walking.

"*No.*"

I nodded. I could see her face, pale even in the wan light of the lamp.

"How did you know?"

I shook my head. "I haven't got time to go into that now. A man's life is at stake. Come on, V, we need to get on. There'll be time for explanations later."

She looked stubborn but I didn't give her time to argue. We reached the village and raced up the high street to the welcoming lights and noise of The Brown Cow.

Of course, I had never set foot in there before. I'd never been inside a public house in my life. I hesitated on the doorstep but then Verity took my arm and swept me inside as if she owned the place.

I spotted the inspector straight away. He sat at the bar with a newspaper in front of him and a pint of ale in his hand. He looked up as we approached and a strange mixture of emotions seemed to cross his face. He looked at once apprehensive, annoyed, eager and hopeful.

"Miss Hart. And Miss Hunter," he said, looking from one of us to the other. "What a pleasant, not-entirely-unexpected surprise. What can I do for you?"

Chapter Twenty Two

It was half past ten by the time Verity and I got back to Merisham Lodge. Verity immediately sped upstairs to check on Dorothy. I walked into the kitchen expecting to find it empty, to be surprised by the sight of Mrs Watling sitting at the kitchen table. I was touched to think she'd waited up for me.

"Joan. Are you feeling better?" She got up and came closer. She looked worried, and for a moment I felt very bad about deceiving her, the good woman that she was.

"Yes, I'm feeling much better, thank you. The doctor gave me some medicine." I didn't want to look her in the face as I lied.

"You still look awfully pale. I think you should go straight up to bed."

I couldn't tell her that my pallor came from apprehension – and possibly excitement. "I must just get the kitchen ship-shape before I go up."

Mrs Watling glanced about. "Maggie and I have done most of it."

I put a hand on her arm, trying to inject as much sincerity into my voice as I could. I could not afford for her to stay in this kitchen, not tonight. "Really, Mrs Watling. I'll just do the last little bits and then I promise I'll turn in for the night. Why don't you go? Go and get some rest."

She took a little bit more persuasion but eventually I saw her off to her room with a 'good night'. After she had gone, I stood there in the middle of the floor, fizzing. I wiped my forehead with shaking hands, took a deep breath and then turned and made for the staircase.

The house seemed so silent. It could have been the early hours of the morning, so still and quiet were the rooms and corridors. I walked softly but quickly along the passageway towards the study, knowing I had to do this right now before I lost my nerve.

The door to the study was shut but the internal window gave out a soft glow of light. I paused outside the door for a moment, trying to control my breathing. My hands were shaking, and I smoothed them down my apron again and again, trying to stop the movement. I had to look calm, I had to look purposeful, otherwise it wouldn't work. I took a final deep breath and then opened the door.

Rosalind Makepeace looked up in surprise as I

entered the room. She was alone, sat at the desk to the right side of the fireplace, her glossy dark hair pinned smoothly back from her face.

"Joan," she said. "What is it?"

I surprised myself by the firmness of my voice. "I was just wondering if you wanted more tea, miss?"

If she was surprised at the undercook asking her that question, she didn't show it. Her brows drew down in a slight frown but she answered quite civilly. "No. No, thank you."

My heart was thumping so hard I was surprised I could hear myself over its beats. "Are you sure I can't get you anything, miss?"

Rosalind was looking at me properly now. "No," she said after a moment.

I drew closer to the desk, close enough so I could rest the tips of my fingers on the edge of it. Rosalind stared at me. "Nothing at all?" She said nothing. I leant a little further in and said "Nothing from the root cellar, for instance?"

There was a moment's silence. I saw her face flicker with an emotion that was quickly suppressed. I waited.

"What on Earth do you mean?" she asked eventually. Her face was blank but her voice betrayed her with the slightest tremor.

I leant ever further forward, fixing her with my gaze. "I saw you," I said, quietly. "I saw you down there on the day Peter Drew died."

She said nothing. I could see the pupils of her eyes shrink down to pinpoints, even in the dim light. "I don't know what you mean," she said, eventually.

"No?" I straightened up. It was wicked of me but I was almost enjoying this. "I'm sure I could jog your memory."

I saw her throat ripple as she swallowed. Then she tore her gaze from mine and bent her head down again. "Joan, you're deluded. I have no idea what you're talking about," she said, trying for a bored tone but not quite able to master it.

"Well," I said, leaning forward again. "I'll give you an hour to think about it. Perhaps your memory will come back. You can find me down in the kitchen if you want to...talk about *arrangements*."

I left then. I thought that was as good a line as any.

I hurried back down the corridor, trying not to look over my shoulder. The house seemed more than ordinarily full of creaks and whispers. I walked down the stairs to the kitchen, trying not to flinch at the sound of my footsteps on the boards. Would what I had done be enough? Surely it would. If what I had surmised was correct, there was no way that a threat such as the one I had just made could be ignored.

I reached the kitchen and checked that the back door was unlocked. For a moment, I stood in the middle of the floor, unsure of what to do. My eye fell on the knife block and I picked it up and moved it into the pantry. I had a nasty moment when I thought someone was hiding by the larder but it was just the shadow cast by an apron hanging from the hook on the wall.

I had to look busy. I had to *keep* busy, otherwise my nerve would go completely. I picked up a cloth and began wiping the already clean table-top with quick, nervous swipes.

Outside in the corridor I heard the tinkle of one of the bells. *Verity's signal*. My heart felt as if it had leapt up into my throat. I moved to the sink, unable to turn my back fully to the doorway.

Above the thumping of the blood in my ears, I heard footsteps coming down the stairs. Quiet footsteps, as if the person walking down was trying not to be heard. I realised I was holding my breath. I turned more fully towards the doorway and saw the long black shadow falling over the threshold. My heart hammered.

"Oh, Joan," said Duncan Cartwright, coming into the kitchen. He looked very big against the light from the corridor. I turned so my back was against the kitchen sink, trying to smile, trying to look innocent and unconcerned. I couldn't stop my gaze falling to his hands, which, thank God, were empty.

"You're up late," he said, smiling, walking forward. We faced each other across the kitchen table.

"I'm just off up to bed, sir." I braced my trembling fingers against the cold porcelain of the sink behind me.

Duncan looked about him with curiosity. "I haven't been down here for years. Not for years." He stopped moving forward and I breathed a little better. "I used to come down here all the time when I was a boy."

"Yes sir, I know. Mrs Watling told me."

Duncan was still looking about him. He had a strange look on his face, as if he were in the midst of a not particularly pleasant dream. Like a sleepwalker. "Yes, I used to come down here a lot. It was...safe. It felt like a safe place."

"Yes, sir," I said, sounding stupid. In my plans, I hadn't thought this far ahead as to what I would actually say. Well, I *had* thought it out, but now that it actually came to it, I wasn't sure I could go ahead with it. It was something about Duncan's face, a kind of vulnerability to it. Despite what he had done, I didn't want to hurt him.

He stopped looking around and focused on me then. Something of the dreaminess went out of his face and his expression sharpened. My heart rate sped up a notch. "You've been telling stories, Joan."

I cleared my throat. "I know what I saw, sir."

"So Rosalind tells me. She said you saw something."

"Yes." I could feel a thin trickle of sweat beginning to inch its way down my spine.

Duncan's face darkened. "What do you want?"

I know I was supposed to say 'money' but the word stuck in my throat. "I don't want anything, sir."

He came close then, his eyes fixed on my face. I swallowed. "Everybody wants something."

We stared at one another. Part of me wanted to scream but nothing had happened, had it? He hadn't admitted to anything. In a split second, I made up my mind.

"Why did you kill your step-mother?"

The baldness of the statement shocked me. I saw Duncan's face whiten. It was then I realised how utterly exhausted he looked, his eyes ringed with shadow, a smudge of beard growth on his jaw. I was reminded of Rosalind, when she'd come down looking for Mrs Anstells, how wraith-like she had appeared. It was then I had an inkling of just how much this whole affair had cost the two of them. Had it been worth it?

Duncan flexed his fingers. "Don't be ridiculous, Joan. You know I have an alibi for that night."

"No, you don't." I had never spoken like this to any of the family before. "Benton lied to the police about where he was that night. He wasn't bringing you things in the drawing room at all. You had ample time to go to the library and kill Lady Eveline."

A muscle twitched in Duncan's pale cheek. "Oh, so you think you know all about it, do you? A chit like you?" He leant forward. "You – you're nothing. You're *nobody*. Nobody is going to be believe you."

I stared back at him. "I'm not so sure about that."

"Well, they're not going to get the chance." He was trembling, his hands shaking. "You think we're going to stop now, after all we've done?"

This is when I knew I should scream. I tried to but my throat was so dry, all I heard was a click. I couldn't take my eyes from Duncan's face, from his haunted eyes and the lips that were drawing back from his teeth.

"That's what nobody tells you," he said in a whisper. "Once you've done it once, it just gets easier and easier. The first time is the worst. I wasn't expecting the blood. I wasn't expecting that at all. But she didn't make a sound – *not a sound*. One minute she was standing up alive, and the next minute she was dead."

Somehow I managed to force a word out. "Why?"

Duncan raised his trembling hands. "She deserved it," he whispered. "She killed my mother."

Then his hands were around my throat, and the scream that should have been screamed a moment before, saving me, was choked off. Gasping, I scrabbled uselessly, pulling at his hands with fingers that weakened even as I tried to pull free. *I should have screamed before*, was the one thought that kept hammering through my brain, even over the pounding of blood in my ears. *I should have screamed before.*

Then I *was* screaming – no, not me, but somebody was. In my darkening vision, I saw a flash of red hair and then there was a sound like somebody hitting the side of a heavy saucepan with a wooden spoon. The pressure around my throat eased and I slumped downwards to my knees, gasping for air. Then there was shouting and the crash of the kitchen door as it hit the wall, and the sound of heavy boots and more shouting, and amidst it all, I became aware of Verity's arm about me, holding me up, and her voice in my ear saying very calmly, "Don't worry, Joanie, you're safe, you're safe. I've got you now."

Chapter Twenty Three

"THAT WAS EXTREMELY FOOLISH OF you, Miss Hart," Inspector Marks said sharply, when we were finally all sat down in Mrs Watling's parlour. "I told you to let my men know as soon as he entered the room. I didn't expect you to launch some kind of suicidal bid for a confession or I would never have allowed you to do what you did."

I rubbed my throat. "I'm sorry, sir."

"Humph." Inspector Marks continued to glare at me for a moment and then his expression softened. "Brave of you, though, Miss Hart. And you, Miss Hunter."

Verity smiled. "I was going to say I hope I haven't hurt Mr Duncan too much, but I'm afraid that would be a lie."

Inspector Mark's moustache twitched. "He'll live."

Mrs Watling put down her empty sherry glass and hurriedly poured herself a replacement. "But what *happened*?" she asked the room in general.

Verity and I looked at the Inspector. He courteously inclined his head. "I think you ladies have earned the floor. For now. Miss Hart, why don't you start?"

Mr Fenwick, who was sitting in the armchair next to Mrs Anstells, twitched. I think it was at the thought of me, a humble kitchen maid, being allowed to speak freely. I was amazed that he managed to restrain himself from protesting, and that, coupled with a surge of pride, gave me the courage to speak up. I wished my voice just sounded a little firmer and more forthright.

"Well," I began, hesitatingly. "I'm not really sure why I first started suspecting." I faltered, then. It was going to be very hard to speak disparagingly about the family in front of the senior staff.

"Go on, Joan," Verity urged. "You knew as soon as you'd set eyes on Benton and Nora."

I blushed. I had been hoping to keep Nora's name, and especially her condition, out of my narrative, but now I could see that that was going to be impossible. I made a mental note to ask the inspector to urge Mrs Anstells not to give her notice, although I couldn't imagine what was going to become of her. I put that worry to one side for the moment and went on with my speech.

"Well, it suddenly occurred to me that we'd all been thinking that there was just one killer. I was watching...er, Nora and Benton, together at lunch, and despite me knowing of their...er, attachment, even if that had been broken, they acted as if they were invisible to one another. No, not even that, as if they *disliked* one another." I could see by the looks on Mrs Anstells' and Mr Fenwick's faces that they didn't know what I was talking about. I sighed and elaborated. "Nora and Benton had been romantically involved with one another. But the way they acted around one another was as if they actively disliked one another. It was a smokescreen, to camouflage their real feelings. And even after their affection had been broken, they were still acting like that. I suppose it had become second nature."

I rubbed my throat again. It still hurt to talk, but I went on. "I suddenly realised, watching them, that I'd seen Duncan and Rosalind act in exactly the same way. They pretended to dislike each other because actually, they felt exactly the opposite but didn't want anyone to know. Once I'd realised that, it seemed so obvious. There was never just one killer, there were two."

"Shocking," said Mrs Anstells. Mr Fenwick said nothing but shook his head in what I took to be silent denigration of the depravity of human beings.

"Once I realised that there were two people involved, and that Benton might have been with Nora on the night that Lady Eveline was murdered, it was easy to look at alibis and realise that Duncan, on that night, and Rosalind on the night that Peter Drew was killed, didn't actually have watertight alibis after all. Benton lied about his whereabouts because he didn't want to get into trouble. Just like Gladdie never said anything about what she'd seen Lord Cartwright do the night Lady Alice died."

"So Duncan killed his stepmother," said Inspector Marks.

I nodded. "That was the planned killing. I think they killed Peter – I mean, Rosalind killed him – because he'd found out something about the first murder. He was blackmailing Duncan – you remember, Verity, he talked to Dorothy about the money he was coming into?" Verity nodded, her mouth tight. "We thought then it was because he was going to inherit from his mother's estate, but of course we found out that that wasn't the case."

Mrs Watling looked rather sick. She had emptied her second sherry glass. "I would never have believed it. Young Duncan. He was such a sweet little boy. I find it hard to believe he could do such a thing."

"I'm afraid it's true," said Inspector Marks. "He confessed to it. It was a revenge killing, of course. Duncan knew that his father was responsible for the death of his mother, Lady Alice. That must have festered inside him for years, especially when Lord Cartwright married Lady Eveline so quickly after Lady Alice's death."

"Is that what he meant when he said 'she killed my mother'?" I asked. "Lady Eveline?"

The inspector shrugged. "No doubt that's what he thought – that Lady Eveline was in on the plot with his father. It could be true. It could be false. I suppose unless Lord Cartwright comes clean, we might never know."

"Revenge," Mrs Watling said, shaking her head. "What a terrible thing."

"It wasn't just that," said Verity. We all looked at her. She smoothed a wisp of hair back from her face and went on speaking. "Joan and I think Duncan and Rosalind had a much more prosaic reason."

"What is that?" Mrs Watling asked, looking as if she might faint at the thought of an even more depraved motive being revealed.

Verity looked sad. "Money. Duncan knew that if his father were hanged for murder, he would inherit everything. The title, the properties, the land, the whole estate. Then he and Rosalind could do what they liked."

I was nodding. I had known there was a reason that the wills in this case had seemed so important.

Mrs Anstells looked very disapproving. "I cannot believe, Inspector, that you allowed this young girl to put herself in terrible danger. I find it difficult to accept that the police force allow such unorthodox methods."

The inspector looked amused. "Well, I don't

get results by being particularly orthodox, my dear Mrs Anstells. But you're right. I would never have allowed Miss Hart here to go so far in the pursuit of justice if I'd known what she was about."

The four elders looked severely at both me and Verity. I kept my face straight but I could hear Verity's thoughts as clearly as if she were shouting them in my ear. I didn't dare look at her for bursting out laughing.

"It was very forward indeed of you, Joan," said Mr Fenwick, his eyebrows bristling. Then he sighed. "Although we're none of us quite ourselves at the moment. It's been such an unsettled time."

"I should be very sorry to lose Joan," Mrs Watling said unexpectedly. "She's an enormous help to me."

I held my breath. Was I about to be dismissed? Was Mrs Watling softening the blow?

"Well, there won't be any question of her leaving," Mr Fenwick said, sounding rather grumpy about it. "Although, Joan, I hope we never see or hear of you making such a spectacle of yourself ever again. Your place depends on it."

"I understand, sir," I said, trying to sound as demure and respectful as possible.

"The same goes for you, Verity," said Mr Fenwick, glaring at her from under his brows.

"Yes, sir." Verity looked as innocent as it was possible for her to look.

"Well," said the inspector. He took his hat in

his hand and made to stand up. "I hope that this will be the last time we meet, Miss Hart and Miss Hunter." He straightened the sleeve of his suit jacket and shot us both a glance. "But I do wonder. I'll see myself out, Fenwick, and leave you in peace. Hopefully this will be the end to it and you can all get back to normal now."

Later, Verity and I stood at the edge of the terrace, looking out at the gardens. It was a damp, dreary, misty sort of day with little ribbons of mist hanging about the trees. I thought I should be feeling exhilarated, or at least glad, but, truth be told, I felt sort of empty. Sort of flat. I suppose I was just exhausted. My throat really hurt.

"You know what the inspector said about getting back to normal?" asked Verity.

I looked at her. "Yes?"

"Well, it's not really going to happen, is it? I mean, the only one left of the family now is Dorothy, and she won't want to stay *here*. Too many bad memories."

"True," I agreed. "So, it's back to London for us, I suppose?"

"I suppose so. Until everything gets settled."

I sighed. "Another court case."

Verity gave me a nudge with her elbow. "If you want to avoid the court cases, Joanie, you've got to stop catching criminals."

I laughed. "Yes, I suppose so."

We stood silently for a moment, looking out at the dripping verdure. I wondered if Verity was running our recent conversation with the inspector through her mind, just as I was. Something occurred to me.

"Oh, V, what are we going to do about Nora? How can we help her?"

Verity gave me a glance I couldn't interpret. "Don't worry, Joanie. I'll make sure she's all right."

"In what way?"

Verity patted my hand. "Don't you worry about it." She hesitated and then said "I've spoken to Dorothy about it and she's agreed to help her."

"*Dorothy* has?" I couldn't understand it.

Verity nodded. "I'm not sure we'll be able to convince Mrs Anstells to keep Nora on, but we can certainly help with the...the other situation." I didn't really understand what she meant, although I had an inkling.

"Is Dorothy very angry at her?" I asked.

Verity shook her head. "Let's just say she... sympathises."

I turned a shocked face to Verity, who smiled and then shook her head very slightly, letting me understand she wouldn't say any more.

I understood and nodded. We stood there for a moment longer in silence, busy with our own thoughts. Then Verity shivered. "I'll be glad to get back to the old Smoke," she said.

"Yes?" I wasn't so sure, myself. Much as my time at Merisham Lodge had been fraught with danger and distress, I would miss the countryside.

Verity shivered again, theatrically. "Yes. It's too bloody dangerous in the countryside."

I laughed. Then I tucked my arm around hers. "Come on. Let's get a cup of tea before we start work again."

"Good idea." She gave my arm an answering squeeze and we began to walk back to the kitchens, leaving the gardens behind us.

THE END

Enjoyed this book? An honest review left at Amazon, Goodreads, Shelfari and LibraryThing is always welcome and *really* important for indie authors. The more reviews an independently published book has, the easier it is to market it and find new readers.

Want some more of Celina Grace's work for free? Subscribers to her mailing list get a free digital copy of **Requiem (A Kate Redman Mystery: Book 2)**, a free digital copy of **A Prescription for Death (The Asharton Manor Mysteries Book 2)** *and* a free PDF copy of her short story collection **A Blessing From The Obeah Man.**

Requiem (A Kate Redman Mystery: Book 2)

WHEN THE BODY OF TROUBLED teenager Elodie Duncan is pulled from the river in Abbeyford, the case is at first assumed to be a straightforward suicide. Detective Sergeant Kate Redman is shocked to discover that she'd met the victim the night before her death, introduced by Kate's younger brother Jay. As the case develops, it becomes clear that Elodie was murdered. A talented young musician, Elodie had been keeping some strange company and was hiding her own dark secrets.

As the list of suspects begin to grow, so do the questions. What is the significance of the painting Elodie modelled for? Who is the man who was seen with her on the night of her death? Is there any connection with another student's death at the exclusive musical college that Elodie attended?

As Kate and her partner Detective Sergeant Mark Olbeck attempt to unravel the mystery, the dark undercurrents of the case threaten those whom Kate holds most dear...

A Prescription for Death (The Asharton Manor Mysteries: Book 2) – a novella

"I HAD A SURGE OF KINSHIP the first time I saw the manor, perhaps because we'd both seen better days."

It is 1947. Asharton Manor, once one of the most beautiful stately homes in the West Country, is now a convalescent home for former soldiers. Escaping the devastation of post-war London is Vivian Holt, who moves to the nearby village and begins to volunteer as a nurse's aide at the manor. Mourning the death of her soldier husband, Vivian finds solace in her new friendship with one of the older patients, Norman Winter, someone who has served his country in both world wars. Slowly, Vivian's heart begins to heal, only to be torn apart when she arrives for work one day to be told that Norman is dead.

It seems a straightforward death, but is it? Why did a particular photograph disappear from Norman's possessions after his death? Who is the sinister figure who keeps following Vivian? Suspicion and doubts begin to grow and when another death occurs, Vivian begins to realise that the war may be over but the real battle is just beginning...

A Blessing From The Obeah Man

DARE YOU READ ON? HORRIFYING, scary, sad and thought-provoking, this short story collection will take you on a macabre journey. In the titular story, a honeymooning couple take a wrong turn on their trip around Barbados. The Mourning After brings you a shivery story from a suicidal teenager. In Freedom Fighter, an unhappy middle-aged man chooses the wrong day to make a bid for freedom, whereas Little Drops of Happiness and Wave Goodbye are tales of darkness from sunny Down Under. Strapping Lass and The Club are for those who prefer, shall we say, a little meat to the story...

JUST GO TO CELINA'S WEBSITE to sign up. It's quick, easy and free. Be the first to be informed of promotions, giveaways, new releases and subscriber-only benefits by subscribing to her (occasional) newsletter.

http://www.celinagrace.com
Twitter: @celina__grace
Facebook: http://www.facebook.
com/authorcelinagrace

Have you read the first Asharton Manor Mystery?

This is the book that introduces Joan and Verity and it's available as a permanently FREE download:

Death at the Manor (The Asharton Manor Mysteries: Book 1)

Please note – this is a novella-length piece of fiction – not a full length novel

IT IS 1929. ASHARTON MANOR stands alone in the middle of a pine forest, once the place where ancient pagan ceremonies were undertaken in honour of the goddess Astarte. The Manor is one of the most beautiful stately homes in the West Country and seems like a palace to Joan Hart, newly arrived from London to take up a servant's position as the head kitchen maid. Getting to grips with her new role and with her fellow workers, Joan is kept busy, but not too busy to notice that the glittering surface of life at the Manor might be hiding some dark secrets. The beautiful and wealthy mistress of the house, Delphine Denford, keeps falling ill but why? Confiding her thoughts to her friend and fellow housemaid, feisty Verity Hunter, Joan is unsure of what exactly is making her uneasy, but then Delphine Denford dies...

Armed only with their own good sense and quick thinking, Joan and Verity must pit their wits against a cunning murderer in order to bring them to justice.

Download Death at the Manor from Amazon Kindle for free,

Other books by Celina Grace:

THE ASHARTON MANOR MYSTERIES

Some old houses have more history than others...

The Asharton Manor Mysteries Boxed Set is a four part series of novellas spanning the twentieth century. Each standalone story (about 20,000 words) uses Asharton Manor as the backdrop to a devious and twisting crime mystery. The boxed set includes the following stories:

DEATH AT THE MANOR

It is 1929. Asharton Manor stands alone in the middle of a pine forest, once the place where ancient pagan ceremonies were undertaken in honour of the goddess Astarte. The Manor is one of the most beautiful stately homes in the West Country and seems like a palace to Joan Hart, newly arrived from London to take up a servant's position as the head kitchen maid. Getting to grips with her new role and with her fellow workers, Joan is kept busy, but not too busy to notice that the glittering surface of life at the Manor might be hiding some dark secrets. The beautiful and wealthy mistress of the house, Delphine Denford, keeps falling ill but why? Confiding her thoughts to her friend and fellow housemaid Verity Hunter, Joan is unsure of what exactly is making her uneasy, but then Delphine Denford dies... Armed only with their own good sense and quick thinking, Joan and Verity must pit their wits against a cunning murderer in order to bring them to justice.

A Prescription for Death

It is 1947. Asharton Manor, once one of the most beautiful stately homes in the West Country, is now a convalescent home for former soldiers. Escaping the devastation of post-war London is Vivian Holt, who moves to the nearby village and begins to volunteer as a nurse's aide at the manor. Mourning the death of her soldier husband, Vivian finds solace in her new friendship with one of the older patients, Norman Winter, someone who has served his country in both world wars. Slowly, Vivian's heart begins to heal, only to be torn apart when she arrives for work one day to be told that Norman is dead. It seems a straightforward death, but is it? Why did a particular photograph disappear from Norman's possessions after his death? Who is the sinister figure who keeps following Vivian? Suspicion and doubts begin to grow and when another death occurs, Vivian begins to realise that the war may be over but the real battle is just beginning...

The Rhythm of Murder

It is 1973. Eve and Janey, two young university students, are en route to a Bristol commune when they take an unexpected detour to the little village of Midford. Seduced by the roguish charms of a young man who picks them up in the village pub, they are astonished to find themselves at Asharton Manor, now the residence of the very wealthy, very famous, very degenerate Blue Turner, lead singer of rock band Dirty Rumours. The golden summer rolls on, full of sex, drugs and rock and roll, but Eve begins to sense that there may be a sinister side to all the hedonism. And then one day, Janey disappears, seemingly run away... but as Eve begins to question what happened to her friend, she realises that she herself might be in terrible danger...

NUMBER THIRTEEN, MANOR CLOSE

It is 2014. Beatrice and Mike Dunhill are finally moving into a house of their own, Number Thirteen, Manor Close. Part of the brand new Asharton Estate, Number Thirteen is built on the remains of the original Asharton Manor which was destroyed in a fire in 1973. Still struggling a little from the recent death of her mother, Beatrice is happy to finally have a home of her own – until she begins to experience some strange happenings that, try as she might, she can't explain away. Her husband Mike seems unconvinced and only her next door neighbour Mia seems to understand Beatrice's growing fear of her home. Uncertain of her own judgement, Beatrice must confront what lies beneath the beautiful surface of the Asharton Estate. But can she do so without losing her mind – or her life?

Have you met Detective
Sergeant Kate Redman?

THE KATE REDMAN MYSTERIES ARE the
bestselling detective mysteries from Celina Grace,
featuring the flawed but determined female officer
Kate Redman and her pursuit of justice in the West
Country town of Abbeyford.

Hushabye (A Kate Redman Mystery: Book 1)
is the novel that introduces Detective Sergeant Kate
Redman on her first case in Abbeyford. It's available
for free!

**A missing baby. A murdered girl. A case
where everyone has something to hide...**

On the first day of her new job in the West Country, Detective Sergeant Kate Redman finds herself
investigating the kidnapping of Charlie Fullman,
the newborn son of a wealthy entrepreneur and his
trophy wife. It seems a straightforward case... but
as Kate and her fellow officer Mark Olbeck delve
deeper, they uncover murky secrets and multiple
motives for the crime.

Kate finds the case bringing up painful memories of
her own past secrets. As she confronts the truth about
herself, her increasing emotional instability threatens
both her hard-won career success and the possibility
that they will ever find Charlie Fullman alive...

Requiem (A Kate Redman Mystery: Book 2)

THE GIRL'S BODY LAY ON the riverbank, her arms outflung. Her blonde hair lay in matted clumps, shockingly pale against the muddy bank. Her face was like a porcelain sculpture that had been broken and glued back together: grey cracks were visible under the white sheen of her dead skin. Her lips were so blue they could have been traced in ink...

When the body of troubled teenager Elodie Duncan is pulled from the river in Abbeyford, the case is at first assumed to be a straightforward suicide. Detective Sergeant Kate Redman is shocked to discover that she'd met the victim the night before her death, introduced by Kate's younger brother Jay. As the case develops, it becomes clear that Elodie was murdered. A talented young musician, Elodie had been keeping some strange company and was hiding her own dark secrets.

As the list of suspects begin to grow, so do the questions. What is the significance of the painting Elodie modelled for? Who is the man who was seen with her on the night of her death? Is there any connection with another student's death at the exclusive musical college that Elodie attended?

As Kate and her partner Detective Sergeant

Mark Olbeck attempt to unravel the mystery, the dark undercurrents of the case threaten those whom Kate holds most dear...

Requiem (A Kate Redman Mystery: Book 2) is the second in the Kate Redman Mystery series.

Imago (A Kate Redman Mystery: Book 3)

"THEY DON'T FEAR ME, QUITE the opposite. It makes it twice as fun... I know the next time will be soon, I've learnt to recognise the signs. I think I even know who it will be. She's oblivious of course, just as she should be. All the time, I watch and wait and she has no idea, none at all. And why would she? I'm disguised as myself, the very best disguise there is."

A known prostitute is found stabbed to death in a shabby corner of Abbeyford. Detective Sergeant Kate Redman and her partner Detective Sergeant Olbeck take on the case, expecting to have it wrapped up in a matter of days. Kate finds herself distracted by her growing attraction to her boss, Detective Chief Inspector Anderton – until another woman's body is found, with the same knife wounds. And then another one after that, in a matter of days.

Forced to confront the horrifying realisation that a serial killer may be preying on the vulnerable women of Abbeyford, Kate, Olbeck and the team find themselves in a race against time to unmask a terrifying murderer, who just might be hiding in plain sight...

THE HOUSE ON FEVER STREET is the first psychological thriller by Celina Grace.

Thrown together in the aftermath of the London bombings of 2005, Jake and Bella embark on a passionate and intense romance. Soon Bella is living with Jake in his house on Fever Street, along with his sardonic brother Carl and Carl's girlfriend, the beautiful but chilly Veronica.

As Bella tries to come to terms with her traumatic experience, her relationship with Jake also becomes a source of unease. Why do the housemates never go into the garden? Why does Jake have such bad dreams and such explosive outbursts of temper?

Bella is determined to understand the man she loves but as she uncovers long-buried secrets, is she putting herself back into mortal danger?

The House on Fever Street is the first psychological thriller from writer Celina Grace – a chilling study of the violent impulses that lurk beneath the surfaces of everyday life.

Shortlisted for the 2006 Crime Writers' Association Debut Dagger Award.

References

I found a number of memoirs, reference books and biographies invaluable when researching the history and culture of the 1930s. These include the following:

Knowing Their Place: Domestic service in twentieth-century Britain – Lucy Delap

The Cook's Tale – Nancy Jackman with Tom Quinn

Her Ladyship's Girl: A Maid's Life in London – Anwyn Moyle

The Lady's Maid: My Life in Service – Rosina Harrison

Below Stairs – Margaret Powell

Life Below Stairs: True Lives of Edwardian Servants – Alison Maloney

Extra Special Thanks Are Due To My
Wonderful Advance Readers Team...

THESE ARE MY 'SUPER READERS' who are kind
enough to beta read my books, point out my more
ridiculous mistakes, spot any typos that have
slipped past my editor and best of all, write honest
reviews in exchange for advance copies of my work.
Many, many thanks to you all.

If you fancy being an Advance Reader, just drop
me a line at celina@celinagrace.com and I'll add
you to the list. It's completely free, and you can
unsubscribe at any time.

Acknowledgements

MANY THANKS TO ALL THE following splendid souls:

Chris Howard for the brilliant cover designs; Andrea Harding for editing and proofreading; Tammi Lebrecque for virtual assistance; lifelong Schlockers and friends David Hall, Ben Robinson and Alberto Lopez; Ross McConnell for advice on police procedural and for also being a great brother; Kathleen and Pat McConnell, Anthony Alcock, Naomi White, Mo Argyle, Lee Benjamin, Bonnie Wede, Sherry and Amali Stoute, Cheryl Lucas, Georgia Lucas-Going, Steven Lucas, Loletha Stoute and Harry Lucas, Helen Parfect, Helen Watson, Emily Way, Sandy Hall, Kristýna Vosecká, Katie D'Arcy and of course my lovely Chris, Mabel, Jethro and Isaiah.

Printed by Amazon Italia Logistica S.r.l.
Torrazza Piemonte (TO), Italy